MOLLY'S TALE

THE MARSTONE SERIES - A COMPANION NOVEL

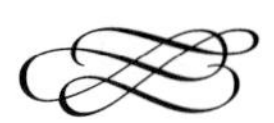

JAYNE DAVIS

Verbena
Books

Copyright © 2021 by Jayne Davis

All rights reserved.

No part of this book may be reproduced in any form or by any electronic or mechanical means, including information storage and retrieval systems, without written permission from the author, except for the use of brief quotations in a book review.

Manuscript development: Elizabeth Bailey

Copyediting & proofreading: Sue Davison

Cover Design: P Johnson

ACKNOWLEDGEMENTS

Thanks to my critique partners on Scribophile for comments and suggestions, particularly Jim, Ysobel and Lola.

Thanks also to Beta readers Tina, Cilla, Dawn, Doris, Frances, Helen, Kristen, Melissa, Patricia, Sarah, and Sue.

CHAPTER 1

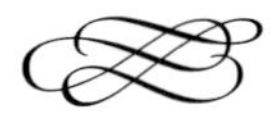

Hertfordshire, June 1782

It was raining when I set off back to Marstone Park at the end of my afternoon off, and not very warm for June, so I hunched into my cloak and walked fast. As I turned into the road leading to the main gates, I heard the hoofbeats and rumble of a carriage behind me and hopped aside just in time. A wheel splashed water from a rut as it passed, soaking the verge beside me in muddy water, but I caught sight of two women inside, one with powdered hair dressed high. The two footmen sitting on the bench at the rear were swathed in cloaks with their hats pulled down. Jem Langton gave me a nod, as he would have done to anyone he recognised; Harry Barlow looked at me with something between a leer and a laugh as he saw me cowering in the hedge. He probably thought the water had hit me.

Up ahead, the coach turned between the stone pillars at the entrance to the estate. I walked faster, keen to find out who was in the coach. It had gone off to Nottingham a few days ago, and Lady Cerney lived near there—one of Lord Marstone's sisters. If it had been her I'd seen, that likely meant that Lady Isabella would be off to London to find a husband. She'd turned eighteen this year, so it was time. And that could be why there was talk in the servants' hall about the London house being opened up.

The likes of me don't get to use the main drive, so I walked on until I came to the rear entrance to the Park. I had more of a spring in my step now—if Lady Isabella was to go to London, I might be as well! Ma had gone there to work as a seamstress when she was twenty—my age now. Wanting some excitement, she said. London certainly sounded more interesting than anything I'd ever seen or done, even though her stories had been accompanied by warnings of the dire things that could happen to a young woman there. She stayed for five years before returning to Over Minster between jobs. The village wheelwright proposed to her, and she never went back to London.

I didn't get a chance to see who had come because, by the time I reached the house, the coach had already been unloaded and taken to the stable yard. My cloak was dripping, so I left it in the room by the servants' door, and my pattens and bonnet, too. Mud on the road had reached the bottom of my skirt, but it was one of the old, drab ones I used to wear when I was only a chambermaid, so I'd have to change anyway before attending Lady Isabella.

"Simons!" the housekeeper called out as I passed her door. A body couldn't even get to her room without being ordered about in this place!

"Mrs Williamson." I gave a curtsey as I stepped into her room. I couldn't think of anything I'd done wrong.

She ran her eye down my person, her face as sour as usual, but only sniffed at my damp cap and hem. "Lady Isabella is to dine with his lordship and Lady Cerney, and you are to make sure she is attired suitably."

"Yes, ma'am." It *had* been Lady Cerney! And if Lady Isabella was summoned to dine with her, it *must* mean we were bound for London.

Mrs Williamson nodded and turned back to the papers on her desk. The clock on her wall showed I had plenty of time to change my gown and help Lady Isabella, but I should get on with it. Better to have her ready early rather than risk her being late. *She* wouldn't blame me, but his lordship would be angry with her, and no-one wanted to have to listen to one of his rants.

I met Jem Langton on the stairs, his dark green livery still a little damp from the journey. He put a hand in his pocket and took out a sealed letter, holding it close to his body so no-one coming upon us would see it. "One of the grooms went over to Nether Minster yesterday—gave me this for Lady Isabella just now."

It wouldn't do for anyone else to see me with it, so I quickly pushed it down into the top of my stays. Barlow would have tried to see down my gown, but Jem's eyes flicked away from my hand as soon as he saw where I was putting the note. He had better manners than Barlow, but didn't seem to be interested in me in that way, more's the pity.

"D'you know why Lady Cerney's come?" I asked. Guessing and hoping were all very well, but I could be wrong.

"I've only heard what you have, Moll." He set off down the stairs. A smile would have been nice—he had a lovely smile, when I'd seen it.

"Do you think it's to do with Marstone House being opened up?" I asked, before he'd taken more than a few steps. I really did want to know; I wasn't only trying to get him to talk to me more. Not this time.

He paused and looked back at me. "We'll find out soon enough." Then he peered down his nose, although one corner of his mouth twitched. "It's not our position to speculate about our betters."

I couldn't help giggling, and he winked. He didn't always act like he'd been starched, and was good at imitating. That had sounded exactly like Benning, the butler, in spite of Jem being thirty years younger—only a few years older than me. "You can listen, can't you?" I said.

"I'm sure I'll overhear something during dinner."

I watched him run down the stairs. From behind, there was hardly any difference between him and Barlow—the same height, both with broad shoulders and nicely muscled calves. According to Ma, it was fashionable to have footmen who looked like twins. They looked similar from the front, too, when both were dressed in their fine livery and powdered wigs, and wearing their correct expressionless faces. If you looked at *them*, though, instead of their clothing and wigs, they clearly weren't the same. Barlow's mouth was narrower, his nose longer, and he usually had a bit of a curl to his lips—a sneer, not a laugh. And the way he looked at me… any of the young maids, really… gave me the shivers.

Jem, though…

Ma told me more than once that a handsome face didn't mean a handsome character, but Jem had been kind to me when I first started here. I'd felt awfully lost in such a huge house and not knowing anyone. He'd found me crying behind the dairy one day—I can't remember now what had distressed me—and had taken me to see the litter of kittens the stable cat had just produced. After that, he'd looked out for me for a while, directing me when I went the wrong way in the many corridors and stairwells, and carrying heavy trays or jugs if he happened to be going the same way. Barlow never did that, nor any of the others.

And Jem never looked at the maids in the way Barlow did.

I hurried up to my room in the attics to change out of my muddy skirt. My hair was still damp, but I stuffed it all into a clean cap before descending to Lady Isabella's room.

She was standing at the window, and turned with a smile as I walked in. "How is your mother, Molly? Did you enjoy your afternoon?"

"She's much better, thank you, my lady." Ma had had a summer cold the last time I'd been home. "We had a nice talk. She's taking in sewing again, now the curate got her them spectacles."

"That's good."

"It's time to get ready for dinner, my lady. You're to dine with his lordship and Lady Cerney, Mrs Williamson said." Best if I kept the letter until she was dressed, or I could end up sending her down late.

She sighed. "Let us select a gown, then."

Some young ladies might be glad to dine with their father, but not in this household. She was summoned to see him once a month, to be questioned about her progress in her lessons. Apart from her governess and the servants, the poor girl hadn't seen anyone else since the twins, her sisters, went to London last year.

Her wardrobe hadn't been attended to for several years, so it didn't take long to choose. There were plenty of plain round gowns that she wore with her governess, but not many nicer ones that still fitted. She was a little thing—short, that is—I was half a head taller than her. But she was pretty, with dark hair and blue eyes.

The yellow and white gown would do nicely, and I pulled it from the closet and held it up. "The stomacher on this is wide enough to fit without having to lace you too tight." She had a full figure—much more in front than I had. I spared a glance down at my own neckline —would Jem take more notice of me if I had more there?

But I was supposed to be helping Lady Isabella. "Pity that blue gown's too small now—that went lovely with your eyes."

Lady Isabella wasn't taking much interest in the gowns. "Molly, is there any talk in the servants' hall about why my aunt has come?"

"Not yet, my lady." I laid the gown on the bed and began to unlace her. "I'll be sure to let you know if I hear anything. But there *is* talk about opening up Marstone House."

Lady Isabella suddenly looked happier. She'd worked out what it all meant, too.

She stepped into the underskirt I held out. I fastened the tapes then helped her into the overdress and pinned the stomacher.

His lordship's other sister had chaperoned Lady Isabella's sisters last year. Lady Cerney must be here instead because neither of the twins had married the men the earl had chosen. He hadn't been pleased—no-one could doubt that, the way he took his temper out on anyone within reach.

The gown was finally on, and I arranged the skirts. "There, my lady. It looks well on you." It did, although it wasn't quite long enough and the sleeves were too tight. I pulled the stool out from under the dressing table and she sat down so I could start on her hair.

"I got this for you, my lady." I gave her the packet, and she took it eagerly, then frowned.

"How long have you had this, Molly?"

"Langton only just gave it to me, my lady, on my way up. Didn't want you trying to read it while I was dressing you!" That might have been a bit overfamiliar, but I was the only person she'd had to chat to since her sisters went away and I'd got used to being able to say what I thought. Lord Wingrave—her brother and his lordship's heir—had been forbidden to come to the Park since his marriage, or even to write to his sisters. I don't know why he was banned—he'd married the woman his lordship picked for him. But from what Lady Isabella had let drop when reading letters from him or her sisters, his marriage was a happy one. He must have bested his father somehow. It was Lord Wingrave who'd arranged for the vicar in Nether Minster to receive letters for my lady and get them smuggled into the Park.

Lady Isabella met my eyes in the mirror and smiled, then broke the seal. "It's from Lizzie." I brushed and pinned her hair while she read it; her face in the mirror looked happy while reading her sister's news, but at the end of it she dropped her hands into her lap and the smile went. She must have been wondering if she would be lucky enough to find a husband she could love.

I put the last pin in. "There, my lady."

She turned her head this way and that to inspect my work in the mirror, then thanked me.

"Dinner's in half an hour—but best to hide that soon in case someone comes for you early." I took her discarded gown into the dressing room for brushing. Lady Isabella followed me in.

"Molly, can Langton listen at the door?"

"I already suggested that, my lady." She left, and I hung up the gown and tidied the dressing room.

I'd missed servants' dinner, having set off for Ma's as it was being served, so as soon as I finished tidying I headed downstairs to scrounge some food. They were busy in the kitchens, cleaning up after preparing his lordship's meal. By the time I felt I could interrupt to ask for something, footmen had started to bring serving dishes and used crockery back. His lordship hadn't taken long over dinner.

"Lady Isabella's ringing for you, Molly." It was the junior maid whose job it was to listen for the bells, and see which one it was before it stopped moving. My stomach growled as I headed for the stairs—no food for me yet!

When I reached her room, Lady Isabella was pulling the pins out of her stomacher, dropping some on the floor in her hurry. Her face was flushed.

"My lady?" What had happened at dinner to put her into this state?

"Molly, find my disguise." She removed the remaining pins then shrugged out of the overdress and let it fall to the floor. "I want to listen at the service door in the blue parlour, but I can't risk being seen in the corridors in my normal clothes."

"Langton will be serving there, my lady." I was burning to know what had been said at dinner—if Lady Isabella was to go to London, would I go too? But there was no time now to ask; she was in too much of a hurry to find out more herself.

The things she wanted were bundled up in the bottom of the clothes press—an old gown of mine from my days as a chambermaid, let out to fit her, and a cap. This wouldn't be the first time she'd tried eavesdropping. Most unladylike, but she wasn't the type to meekly wait to be informed what she must do.

"Papa will send him out. I'll need you to show me the way, though —I've only listened at the library door before."

Anyone who saw her close-to couldn't fail to recognise her, but in my clothes she might not be identified from a distance. I helped her on with the drab gown, then twisted her hair into a knot and covered it with the cap. "I'll bring a tisane up and say you're not to be disturbed."

The top of the servants' stair in this wing wasn't far from her door. I led the way down and into the dim passage that ran alongside the parlours at the front of the house.

"That's it." I kept my voice to a whisper and pointed to a sliver of light where the servants' door had been left open a little. Jem's doing, probably. He'd have guessed that Lady Isabella would want to listen. "If anyone opens it, go further on. The door to the breakfast room is the next one along. You might be able to get back to your room that way." These corridors only had a few lamps to help us find the right doors—my lady could easily get lost trying to find her own way back through the servants' passages and end up by the butler's room. The game would be up then, and no mistake.

I went to the kitchens to request the tisane, and took it up to Lady Isabella's room—that would be excuse enough if anyone asked where she was. Then it was nearly time for supper, and I really didn't want to miss that.

I'd not been in the servants' hall long when Jem came in. The menservants sat further up the table, but he stopped on the way past. "It sounded like Lady Isabella will be going to London. There was talk at dinner about a dancing master and her being introduced. I was sent out of the blue parlour before his lordship and Lady Cerney got talking."

"Ooh, that'll be exciting."

Barlow overheard. "What makes you think you'll be going, Molly?" His lip curled in that horrible way he had. "You're not a proper lady's maid, and you don't know anything about London. You won't be any use."

I looked around, trying to keep dismay from showing on my face. It was true—I had no proper training. Betsy had looked after the three young ladies for years, and I'd helped her now and then. Betsy went to London with the twins last year, and she stayed with Lady Elizabeth when she married. I'd heard she was wed to Lady Elizabeth's butler now—something that could never happen here, as his lordship didn't allow any of his staff to be married.

When Betsy didn't return to Marstone Park, Mrs Williamson said I might as well carry on looking after Lady Isabella. It seemed no-one thought it was worth her having a properly trained maid, poor lass. But I wasn't complaining—it got me out of emptying slops and making up fires. I suppose it wouldn't be too bad to go back to that—

I'd still have a job close enough to visit Ma on my days off. The problem was, I'd ended up in the position of Lady Isabella's personal maid ahead of girls, and women, who'd been in service here for much longer. They'd have loved to see me back at their level, and could make my life very unpleasant if they chose to.

I reached for another bit of cheese—there was nothing to be gained by missing my supper, and I'd soon find out from Lady Isabella what was to happen. I'd think of something to get them to take me, too.

CHAPTER 2

Lady Isabella didn't say much when I undressed her that night, only that she *was* to go to London with her father and Aunt Aurelia—Lady Cerney, that is. Lady Cerney was being paid to find her a suitable match and didn't like Lady Isabella's father; that last bit wasn't surprising, as I'd never heard of anyone who did.

I didn't ask who was to be her maid. For one thing, she had more important things on her mind and probably hadn't thought about it. For another—if she asked for me to go with her, Lord Marstone was likely to say no out of spite. He was that kind of man.

But I gave it some thought overnight. There was more to the world than Marstone Park and Over Minster, and going to London with my lady might be the only way I'd get to see any of it. As well as Ma's stories, I'd heard about London from some of the maids and footmen who moved between the earl's house there and here at the Park, depending on where the family was.

I carried out my plan the next morning, before I could think better of it. Miss Tamworth, Lady Cerney's personal maid, hadn't been at supper yesterday, nor yet at breakfast this morning, so I couldn't find out from her when would be a good time to ask if Lady Cerney would see me. I couldn't afford to wait—Lady Isabella was due to set off to

London that afternoon—so I summoned up my courage and knocked on the parlour door.

"Come!"

I went in, dropping a deep curtsey. Lady Cerney was sitting with a book in her lap. She looked years younger than her brother, although I don't think she was much different in age. Most likely because she still had her figure, and although there were a few signs of wrinkles beneath the powder and paint, she didn't have jowls and broken veins like his lordship. Her gown was something to behold—much fancier than anything I'd ever seen. The fabric was cream, but with embroidered patterns all over, of leaves and flowers twining around each other. Ma never got to sew fancy stuff like that.

"Yes?" She looked down her nose, and I nearly giggled—it reminded me of Jem yesterday, pretending to be the butler. I wasn't given to laughing in front of my betters, but her stern look made me nervous.

"If you please, my lady, I am Molly Simons, Lady Isabella's maid."

She didn't speak, just raised one eyebrow.

"I wished to know, my lady, if I am to go with Lady Isabella." I managed not to fidget with my hands.

"Why should you not? Is she dissatisfied with you?"

"No, my lady." I explained how I came to have my current position. "I'm very quick to learn, my lady."

She shook her head. "Tamworth has enough to do without training you up as well. No—there will be a maid at Marstone House who can look after Isabella until I can find someone more suitable."

Her gaze returned to her book. I remembered what my lady had told me last night—that Lady Cerney seemed to dislike the earl as much as everyone else, and was being paid to take Lady Isabella to London.

I took a deep breath. So far nothing I said had gone as far as outright impertinence, but what I was about to say could lose me my position, and make things worse for Lady Isabella, too.

"If you please, my lady, is Miss Fothergill to accompany you?"

Lady Cerney looked like she'd stepped in something unpleasant. I hurried on before I lost my nerve, and my words came out in a gabble. "It's just… she will report everything… everything you do or say back to Lord Marstone."

She'd been about to send me off, I knew it, but she put her book aside. "What makes you think that?"

"His lordship wants to know everything Lady Isabella does, and Foth— Miss Fothergill reports to him regularly."

"Hmm. I haven't met her yet, but there will be little time for lessons of the kind she can supply." Her eyes narrowed, as if she was judging me again. That must have been why she was getting lines on her face—too much squinting. "Whether or not the governess accompanies us seems to have little bearing on your own position. Why should I take an untrained maid?"

"I won't be tattling, my lady."

"Neither would a new maid." Her brows drew together. "But I would not be this person's employer, Marstone would," she said, as if she was talking to herself. She wasn't stupid—she'd worked it out before I had to explain.

"Mr Staverton—that's his lordship's secretary, my lady—Mr Staverton would give orders to—"

"Yes, yes—I get the point." She pointed a finger at me. "You are also Lord Marstone's employee. He would dismiss anyone he finds disloyal. Are you not afraid of losing your position?"

Lord Wingrave had promised to find employment for anyone dismissed by the earl for helping his sisters, but it wouldn't do for Lady Cerney to know that.

"I'm likely to lose it anyway, my lady, if I am not to go with Lady Isabella."

"Very well. There will be people enough at Marstone House reporting back, without adding another."

"If you please, my lady…" I wondered—again—if I was about to make a great mistake, but I said it anyway. "I know for certain one of the footmen will not do that, either."

Her eyebrows went up. They got a lot of use, those eyebrows. "Taken a fancy to him, have you?"

"I..." My face got hot. "I mean, I haven't done anything improper, and nor has he." Not even a kiss, more's the pity. And it wasn't any liking for me that kept Jem Langton from tattling. He had his eye on the future, when Lord Wingrave became the next earl.

"One step out of line and you will find yourself dismissed without a character. Is that clear?"

"Yes, my lady." I didn't think Lord Wingrave's promise to find us employment included being dismissed for improper conduct.

"His name?"

"Langton, my lady."

"Very well. Pack Lady Isabella's things, and your own. We leave at three o'clock this afternoon. And find Tamworth and send her to me."

I curtseyed, but she had already returned to her book.

After I'd found Tamworth and given her the message from Lady Cerney, I went to finish the packing I'd started that morning, while it was too early for Lady Cerney to be awake. Lady Isabella was writing a letter, so I didn't disturb her.

She sanded the letter and sealed it, then brought it into the dressing room. She looked at my own little bag lying open on the floor. "Are you to come with me, Molly?"

"Yes, my lady."

"Oh, that's good." She did look happy at the news—I'd thought she'd be pleased, but I hadn't been sure. That was gratifying, but it wasn't right that I was the only person she could confide in. "I explained about people reporting to his lordship. Lady Cerney will ask for Langton to be one of the footmen to accompany us."

"Oh, well done!" She handed me the letter. "This is for Will—I mean, Lord Wingrave—to tell him what is happening. Do you think Langton can get it delivered as soon as we get to London?"

"I'll see he gets it, my lady."

"Will probably has someone in Marstone House, so he might already know it's being opened up, but I thought it best to write to him anyway. I do hope I—"

She stopped as someone knocked on the door; I opened it to find Miss Tamworth waiting. Lady Cerney's maid looked to be a similar age to her employer; however, without the powder and paint that Lady Cerney wore, the beginnings of wrinkles were more obvious. She was finely dressed, much finer than any of the servants at Marstone Park. Apart from the footmen in their livery, of course.

Miss Tamworth ignored me, and curtseyed to Lady Isabella. "My lady, I've been sent to help Simons pack your things." She sniffed, her lips pursed. "Your governess stopped me on the way, and said I was to tell… I mean, she requests your presence in the schoolroom, my lady."

Perhaps she was annoyed with Fothergill, not because she had to help me. I hoped so.

Lady Isabella rolled her eyes.

"Fothergill *isn't* going," I whispered as she passed me on her way out. She gave a little smile that Miss Tamworth didn't see.

Miss Tamworth looked me up and down, much as Lady Cerney had. I needed to be careful here—Miss Tamworth would have her mistress' ear, and it would not do to be impertinent or anger her in any way.

"Want to be a lady's maid, do you?"

"I want to be Lady Isabella's maid." I folded my hands in front of me and met her eyes briefly before looking down.

"Hmpf. Lady Cerney told me of your background. She's expecting me to train you."

"I'm sorry for the extra work, Miss Tamworth. But I will learn quickly."

"Just Tamworth will do." She walked around me. "Where did you get the gown?"

"This one used to belong to Lady Theresa. She gave it to me when she went to London last year." It was only one of her round gowns for wearing in the schoolroom, and a practical dark brown. I had others, made using fabric from Lady Isabella's outgrown gowns.

"It fits you well."

That almost sounded like praise. "My mother does sewing, and she helped me to adjust it, and remove a lot of the trimmings."

"You know your station then." She nodded, and her stern expression softened a little.

I kept my face blank. Knowing my station had nothing to do with it—leaving the various ruffles and braiding on would have earned me spiteful comments and, like as not, pinches or trips in the corridors from the girls who thought they should have had my place.

"You speak well."

For an untrained country girl, I guessed she meant. "Thank you. Betsy, the previous lady's maid, told me that I should try to improve my speech. I have tried to copy the way the housekeeper and butler speak." And Lady Isabella, but Tamworth might think that was presumptuous.

"Can you read?"

"Yes." Luckily, she didn't ask how well. I'd had some learning in the village school, and Ma and my brother Tom sometimes had a newspaper to read, but the words didn't come easily to me.

"You were not at supper last night, nor breakfast."

"I eat in the servants' hall." I thought it was Tamworth who'd missed her meals.

Her brows rose, making her look unnervingly like Lady Cerney. "Not with the upper servants? Most unusual. I suppose it's because Lady Isabella is only a daughter of the house."

I should have been eating with Mrs Williamson and Benning? And his lordship's valet? I was very happy *not* to have had my position recognised in that way.

"That will not do," she went on. "Putting you in the servants' hall reflects on my own position."

I was about to say I wasn't a proper lady's maid, but thought better of it. Best not to give her, or anyone else, an excuse to leave me behind. "When we get to London—"

She nodded sharply, once. "Yes, we will start there as we mean to go on. Now, show me what gowns Lady Isabella has. My lady suggested a complete new wardrobe might be required."

I'd already packed most of them, with Lady Isabella's chambermaid disguise at the bottom of the largest trunk. How could I explain that, if Tamworth found it?

"The best gowns are in here." I pointed to the second trunk. Tamworth took out the top three or four garments, and shook her head.

"If these are the best, there's no need to unpack any more. They will not do at all."

Thank the heavens for that.

She repacked them swiftly, showing me how best to fold them to avoid too many creases, and we were soon finished. Even though Lady Isabella didn't have many gowns, there was so much fabric in them that we filled three large trunks as well as a smaller one.

"I'll get them taken downstairs," I said, as Tamworth took her leave, and went to fetch Jem.

"I can't manage those on my own," Jem said, gazing at the trunks. "You should have said—now I'll have to go and fetch someone else to help."

"Sorry, but I needed to see you alone." I held out Lady Isabella's letter. "My lady wrote this for Lord Wingrave."

Jem put it into his pocket. "He'll get it tonight if he's in London."

And it would take days if he was at his home in Devonshire, but there was no help for it. "Are you to go to London, Jem?"

"I reminded Benning that I come from there, but it's him who'll decide. He'd better make his mind up soon."

Hah—as I was expecting. "I'll have you know, Jem Langton, that you are to go to London, and I have arranged it." I couldn't resist poking him in the chest. "And what's more, I'm going too, and Fothergill is not. Now who's no use?"

He backed off a step. "Hey—it was Barlow who said that, not me! But how did you arrange it?"

"I told Lady Cerney that most of the servants will report everything back to Lord Marstone." I hesitated before asking him my next question, but he and I were supposed to be working together to help Lady Isabella, and if we didn't trust each other, who could we trust?

"Do you know of anyone within Marstone House who might already have got word to Lord Wingrave?"

He shook his head. "There's bound to be someone, but I don't know who. Besides, they'll only know the house is being opened, not who is coming and why."

"The housekeeper must know how many bedrooms need to be aired, and which ones." That should be enough of a clue.

He actually looked impressed, and gave me one of his rare smiles. "I suppose so. You might be some use after all, Moll!"

And that was as close to a compliment as I was likely to get from him. He was pleasant to everyone, and nothing more. Oh, once or twice I'd thought he'd looked at me as if he'd taken a fancy to me, but that was likely just my imagination.

Unfortunately, it was Barlow who Jem fetched to help him with the trunks. Barlow said he was the other footman to be going, but that wasn't surprising, them being a matched pair. They'd heard the orders given to the stable staff—his lordship and the two ladies were to go in the best coach, with me, Tamworth, and his lordship's valet following in the old coach, along with most of the luggage.

Barlow came back alone for the small trunk. "You were a long time up here with Langton," he said, standing a little too close. From where he was, he'd have been able to see down the front of my dress if I hadn't tucked my fichu in well.

I put my nose in the air. "You footmen need detailed directions. What's it to do with you, anyway?"

He rested one hand on the wall beside my head. "Just looking out for you, Molly. Wouldn't want any tales to be told about your goings on, would we, that might get you kept here? Not when we can have a lovely time together in London. I can show you all the interesting places."

Go out alone with him? How slow-witted did he think I was? Although it was tempting to put a knee into him where it would hurt, I couldn't risk causing a fuss—particularly not now. I shrank into myself a little instead, as though I was afraid of him. Well, I was, a bit.

A scream would bring someone running, but could easily get me dismissed as well.

"How about a little kiss to keep me quiet?" He leaned in further, and his breath smelled of the onions he'd had at dinner. But as his face got really close I ducked down under his arm and ran off down the corridor.

He didn't follow me—even a favoured footman would get into trouble if he was seen actually chasing one of the maids. I'd come back for my bag later. Lucky for me the two of them would be riding on the back of the main coach, not in with us maids in the second one. The further away I was from Barlow, the happier I'd be.

CHAPTER 3

It was half-past three by the stable clock, and the two coaches were still standing in front of the main entrance. Tamworth was in the old coach with her eyes closed—taking the chance for a nap, by the looks of it. There was no sign of his lordship or their ladyships. Or his lordship's valet, come to that. But the likes of his lordship were never bothered about keeping servants waiting.

It was pleasant enough, leaning on the outside of the coach; the sky was blue and the air warm, and I was enjoying the feel of the sun on my face. Barlow, loitering behind the best coach, wouldn't dare to bother me with Jem and the drivers and grooms looking on. But by the time another ten minutes had passed, I was beginning to wonder if something had happened, and we might not be going at all.

"Go and find out what's happening," the head coachman said at last, in the direction of the two footmen. Barlow just spat on the ground and looked away, but Jem shrugged and ran up the steps that led to the main front door.

"Nearly ready," he announced when he reappeared. That was a relief. "But we need to unload his lordship's trunks." He swung himself up onto the roof of the best coach. "Barlow, get up here and give me a hand."

The earl wasn't coming? That could only be good. Poor Lady Isabella would have a much nicer time in London without her father there. And so would the rest of us.

The two grooms going with us helped, and they stacked the earl's luggage at the bottom of the steps for someone else to take indoors. The ladies' luggage was on our coach—his lordship would have his trunks on the same coach as he was in, of course. If anything happened to us, it wasn't going to be his lordship who was inconvenienced.

"Why?" I whispered, as Jem paused nearby, wiping the sweat from his forehead with a handkerchief. The two of them were done up in all their fine livery—they must have been very hot.

"Lady Cerney was summoned to see his lordship. They were shouting at each other, then Benning sent for the physician."

That must have been while I was with Tamworth in Lady Isabella's room. "Lost his temper, I suppose, and made himself ill?" Again.

Jem shrugged. It was probably a sin, but I couldn't help hoping his lordship wouldn't be fit to travel *too* soon. The two ladies came down the steps, and Barlow handed them into the front coach and shut the door.

"Get in, Simons!" Tamworth sounded tetchy, so I jumped in. It was the first time I'd been in such a grand carriage, even though it was only the second best one. I stuck my head out of the window to see better, watching the big house get smaller as we moved down the drive. Then we were into the trees that surrounded the estate and I couldn't see it any more.

I was on my way to London! I'd have to write to Ma to let her know, but there'd be plenty of time to think about that later.

We passed through Over Minster and I leaned out, hoping someone I knew might see me in such a grand coach, but the only person I saw was the vicar, and he wouldn't pass on the gossip that Molly Simons had come up in the world.

Then we were past the houses and into the fields where I'd sometimes played when I was young. Before long, more houses appeared beside the road.

"What's this place called?" I asked Tamworth.

"How would I know? I only became Lady Cerney's maid when she married—I've never lived here. Now, tell me what you know about getting stains out of silk."

I couldn't help a sigh, but I tried to answer her questions. She was an ally I needed to keep sweet. But in spite of my good intentions, my attention wandered again to the view from the window. Another town, with a tall spire on its church and a market filling the main street, and more people than I'd yet seen in one place.

"Are we in London already?"

"Good heavens, girl, we've been on the road less than an hour! It'll be a couple more hours, at least."

"What's this town called?"

"I have absolutely no idea! Is this the first time you've been beyond your village?"

"Yes."

Her mouth dropped open for a moment, then she shook her head and let down the window. She stuck her head out and called to the coachman to stop when convenient; soon after, the coach pulled over to the side of a wide bit of road. The groom opened the door.

"Is there room for Simons to ride on the box?" Tamworth asked.

The groom eyed me. "Just about. It'll be a bit of a squeeze, mind."

"Off you go, Simons. I'm sure the driver can name all the villages on the way, and I can have a nap while you pester him."

The groom laughed, but helped me out and up onto the box. He was a kindly man, old enough to be my father, and the second coachman was old enough to be my grandfather. They both treated me like my grandpa used to, as well, telling me all about the places we drove through as if I was still a little girl, but I didn't mind. My gown got a bit dusty, but I didn't mind that, either.

We stopped once to change the horses, and a little after that the groom pointed to our left, across some fields. "That's London now." I couldn't make out details of the buildings from where we were, only that there were an awful lot of them, and quite a few spires sticking up. It was going to feel strange, living in the middle of so many people.

"Why aren't we going there?" I asked, as the driver passed a road that went in the direction of the city.

"Marstone House is in the western part of Town," the coachman said. "Quicker to go around the edge than to get stuck in the busy streets in the middle." He smiled at me. "It's big, is London, Molly."

I could see that. But when we did turn in, I'm sure my mouth must have hung open in amazement. The houses weren't nearly as big as the house at Marstone Park, but there were so many of them all together. Ma had told me about it, but I hadn't imagined anything like this. We slowed right down because the roads were full of hawkers, as well as men and women with barrows, all shouting and calling. And the air stank of coal smoke.

"This is Grosvenor Square now."

The square was surrounded by tall houses made of red brick with white stone around the windows and doors, and it had a railed-off garden in the middle. The coach in front stopped by a very grand entrance, but ours went on to the end of the square, then turned a couple of corners. We stopped by a door in a blank wall, in a narrow street that must be behind the main house. A handful of grooms came out to take the horses, and one of them helped me down from the box.

Tamworth emerged, and sniffed as she looked around her. "I think I can remember my way, although it's a long time since my lady came to this house." She opened the door in the wall and we entered a small garden. It was shadowed now, the sun gone behind the tall buildings all around, but there were rose bushes in bloom and plants enough to show it must get some sunshine.

"There's more greenery than I thought," I said. "What with this and the gardens in the square."

She looked at me and rolled her eyes. "This isn't for the likes of us, Simons. And the garden in the square is only for the families who live here. There are locked gates to keep the common folk out."

Of course. We weren't expected to be seen in the grounds at Marstone Park, either.

"Come on, girl. You'll need to learn your way around, so pay attention. And remember—you're a proper lady's maid here. Stand up straight and try not to gawp."

"Yes, Tamworth."

Inside the house, Tamworth led the way along a stone-flagged corridor, past several doors that I didn't have time to look in. At the top of a set of stairs we went through a baize door, like the ones at Marstone Park, which opened onto the main entrance hall. This place might not be as big as Marstone Park, but it was just as fine. The floor was made of black and white tiles, there was red carpet on the wide staircase, and portraits in gilt frames hung on the walls. Lady Cerney and Lady Isabella were in the hall, talking to a plump woman in a dark gown. Her grey hair was tucked under a frilly white cap, and the chain with keys around her waist told me she was the housekeeper. I didn't recognise either of the men beyond them—the stooped old man must be the butler, and his expression was not at all welcoming. The middle-aged one in livery would be the footman who normally lived here.

The housekeeper turned and set off up the stairs, the two ladies following. Tamworth and I hurried after them, up two flights.

"I've put you in the large front chamber, Lady Cerney," the housekeeper said, opening the door and standing aside to let her ladyship enter. "It has been redecorated since you were last here."

"I should hope so, Mrs Wardle. It's been more than twenty years."

"I hope it is to your taste, my lady." Mrs Wardle spoke as if she hadn't heard Lady Cerney's comment. I suppose that was wise, and I should try to follow suit. What with Lady Isabella never seeing anyone outside the household, I hadn't been around any other ladies and gentlemen—I'd have to watch Mrs Wardle and Tamworth carefully and do as they did.

I peered through the doorway as the housekeeper showed Tamworth the dressing room. The bedchamber was not much bigger than the one Lady Isabella had back at Marstone Park, but I suppose anything larger would take up too much space in these London houses.

The housekeeper curtseyed. "I will have hot water sent up, my lady. Refreshments will be ready in the front parlour in ten minutes. Dinner will be in an hour."

"Very late," Lady Cerney muttered as Mrs Wardle left. I thought that was unfair—it wasn't the housekeeper's fault we'd only just arrived.

We went up another flight of stairs. The corridor here was narrower, and Lady Isabella's room was much smaller than the one she had at Marstone Park, but she seemed pleased with it, and dismissed the housekeeper.

"This is the room I had when I came to London before," she said, crossing to the window. Unlike Lady Cerney's, this looked out of the back of the house.

A banging and bumping made me look out onto the corridor. It was Jem and Barlow with the trunks, followed by a maid with a jug of hot water.

When the trunks had been left, Lady Isabella had a quick wash and I repinned her hair. My lady was just smoothing her gown when there was a knock at the door. Barlow stood there, with my bag in his hand. "If you tell me which is your room, Moll, I'll take your bag up for you."

"I don't know myself yet. Leave it there." That wasn't a lie, although I'd have said the same thing anyway. I wasn't going to tell *him* where I would be. And I'd be sure to bolt the door—I didn't trust the likes of him not to try his chances. Things were easier at Marstone Park, where there were separate stairs for the men and women up to their own parts of the top floor. This place didn't look big enough for that.

He scowled but put the bag down where I said, then rearranged his features into a proper blank expression when Lady Isabella came to the door. "Refreshments are ready in the parlour, my lady."

As Lady Isabella followed Barlow down the main stairs, Tamworth popped out from a door in the corridor I hadn't noticed, being painted the same colour as the wall.

She looked me up and down. "Go and tidy your hair, Simons."

Well, I hadn't expected that, but I went back into Lady Isabella's room and tucked all the loose bits back under my cap. I shook out my skirts, then stood straight to be inspected. To my surprise, Tamworth smiled.

"Much better. When in a new house, I always find it best to ensure the housekeeper and butler appreciate my status. The rest of the staff will take their lead from them. No-one will take a lady's maid seriously if she does not present a tidy and neat appearance. Now, Wardle should be offering us tea and something to eat in her room. And whatever the situation was at Marstone Park, here you are a proper lady's maid. You do not report to her."

"Yes, Miss… I mean, thank you, Tamworth." It felt impertinent to address her that way, but she smiled again.

"Good. As you are so young, respectfulness but not subservience will serve you well."

That disguised door opened onto the service stairs. They were lit only by some glass in the roof, so were quite gloomy in spite of the walls being painted white. "You will need to help Lady Isabella change for dinner," Tamworth went on as we descended. "And ensure she has a suitable gown pressed and ready for tomorrow. You will be going to Lady Cerney's mantua-maker with Lady Isabella. She would not normally take a maid, but I suggested it would be useful for you to see how gowns are made."

And Tamworth could have the day in peace, without being expected to continue my training. But I was possibly being unfair—so far, she had been much friendlier and more helpful than I'd expected, and I'd be a fool if I failed to learn from her.

Mrs Wardle's room was bigger than my lady's bedchamber, with a table in the middle large enough to seat six people, a pair of worn but comfortably padded chairs by the fireplace, and a writing desk in one corner. Most of the walls were taken up with cupboards that reached right up to the ceiling, and a case that held record books. I guessed her bed was behind the curtain that hid the far end of the room.

We sat at the table, and a maid brought in a tray laden with tea things and a plate of biscuits and little cakes. They looked fancier than anything I'd had the chance to eat before.

"A very nice selection, Mrs Wardle," Tamworth said. "Don't you think, Simons?" She glared at me while Mrs Wardle fussed with the tea pot, and I realised I'd been staring.

"Yes, indeed." I was longing to taste them, but waited until I had a cup of tea in front of me. I followed Tamworth's lead and only took one.

The little cakes were sweet seed cakes with added spices, and they tasted lovely. But apart from that, my new position was no more interesting than being in the servants' hall. I listened while the two of them said what they'd been doing for the past twenty years, since Tamworth had last been in this house with Lady Cerney, and managed not to take more than one extra cake even though Mrs Wardle ate four. Then they turned to gossip—much the same as I was used to hearing at Marstone Park, but more polite, and with a pretence that they weren't gossiping about the family at all. I paid more attention then, but didn't find out anything I didn't already know—no-one liked the earl, or his man of business, and although they had some sympathy for the young ladies of the family because of the way his lordship ruled over them, they weren't going to risk their positions by going against his lordship's wishes.

CHAPTER 4

I spent an hour unpacking Lady Isabella's things and arranging them neatly into drawers, shelves, and chests, then it was time to dress her for dinner. When she'd gone down, I took her striped gown to the basement and found the laundry room. In spite of Tamworth's careful folding, there were creases to be pressed out before my lady wore it. I'd done the skirts and had just started on the lace when Jem came in.

"Got a minute, Moll?"

"Right now?" I didn't lift my eyes from the gown, keeping the flat iron moving over the cloth so it didn't scorch the fine threads beneath.

"If you can."

I remembered that I didn't have to answer to anyone other than my lady now, and set the iron with the others on the top of the stove before following Jem out of the back door. The air was still warm in the garden, with a faint scent of roses. The sky was beginning to darken, but there was still plenty of light as we made our way along the gravel path and into the stables. Jem went past the occupied stalls with a muttered warning about where I was putting my feet—as if I didn't know the kinds of things a body could step in around horses.

The man waiting for us at the far end wore a brown suit, neat and clean but not fancy, and his hair was tied back with no powder. Jem gave him a nod of respect, so I guessed he wasn't merely a messenger.

"This is Mr Archer, Moll. He works for Lord Wingrave."

Mr Archer dipped his head a little way, as if I was a person to be respected. "Miss Simons?"

"Yes, sir." I curtseyed. It seemed Lord Wingrave had known we were coming—there'd hardly been time for Jem to get my lady's note to him.

"Lord Wingrave wishes to convey his thanks for the help you have given to Lady Isabella so far," Mr Archer said. "Unfortunately, his lordship has to leave London tomorrow, so he has asked a Mr Carterton to... to look out for Lady Isabella on his behalf. Mr Carterton will need to know of Lady Isabella's movements, if possible."

"You want me to...?" My voice came out as a squeak, and I cleared my throat. Spying on my lady? But that didn't seem right. "I mean, can I tell Lady Isabella this?" She would be worried if she didn't hear from her brother.

"Naturally. However, Lord Wingrave intends to write to explain matters himself. I will get the note to you or Langton tomorrow."

Why hadn't he said that to start with? It might be better not to say anything to my lady until she had the letter from her brother in her hand.

"If you have any news, send to the Dog and Partridge, on Davies Street." Mr Archer looked at Jem. "News about Lady Isabella's movements, or anything else you think I, or Mr Carterton, should know."

Jem nodded. I didn't know where Davies Street was, but I would have to send any messages with Jem anyway, like as not. Footmen could find many more excuses than maids for being away from the house.

"Lady Isabella is to go to a mantua-maker tomorrow," I said. "But I don't know where it is."

"Thank you. News of engagements such as morning calls or balls, and so on, will be the most useful." Mr Archer held out a purse of plain cloth. "You may need to send someone with a message, or have other small expenses connected with this matter. Langton has a similar purse." It was heavy, and clinked. I must have shown my surprise, for he chuckled. "There is not as much there as you might think. It's mainly ha'pennies and farthings—you don't want to be giving street children shillings for taking messages."

That made sense. And I'd not be as worried about someone stealing it if there wasn't much there. I slipped the purse through the gap in my skirts into my pocket.

"That's all for now," Mr Archer said. He nodded and slipped out into the street.

"Jem." I spoke before he could leave. "You said you were helping my lady—with the letters and such—because you had your eye on the time Lord Wingrave inherits."

"Yes. He's very different from Lord Marstone—he thinks of servants as people, not just… just *things* to do as they're told. And dismissed on a whim."

"How do you know all that?" Lord Marstone was a horrible father, but not really that bad as an employer, as long as you could keep out of his way and beneath his notice. It was a question I'd been wondering about for some time. I guessed that Lord Wingrave would be a better master, but only because he was good to his sisters.

"Archer used to work at Marstone Park—do you remember?"

"No—I didn't go there until after Lord Wingrave was married." And I still hadn't set eyes on him.

"Ah, right. Archer was only a groom, but he went with Lord Wingrave to Devonshire. Now he's… I'm not sure exactly. Not a steward, but Lord Wingrave trusts him with a lot of things. His lordship rewards people who serve him well. With responsibilities, I mean, not just with money."

"Is that all you know of him?" One man's promotion didn't seem enough to lead to such a judgement.

"There's only a bit more. Two years ago, when all three young ladies came to Town…" He paused, and I nodded. That was when

Lord Wingrave had first upset his lordship's plans for marrying off my lady's sisters. I'd still been emptying chamber pots then.

"We weren't supposed to let Lord Wingrave into the house, but he called to see Lord Marstone. Many would have pushed their way in, and never mind the consequences to the likes of me, but he didn't. He remembered my name, too, even though it was three years since he'd been at Marstone Park. Archer came to see me later—that's when he asked me to help get letters to the young ladies."

"So you're sure he really will find us a new position if we need it?"

"Sure as I can be."

That would have to do.

"You'd best get back in, Molly. I'll wait a bit."

Mowbray, the London butler, was in the corridor as I slipped into the house. "Where have you been?" He wore the sour face I'd seen earlier, and a smell of something sweet hung about him.

"I stepped outside for a breath of air." Tamworth had said I didn't need to answer to him, but it would be silly to put his back up. "It's very hot in the laundry room, and I've Lady Isabella's gowns to finish pressing."

His expression didn't change. "I will not have any carryings-on with the footmen, Simons. Nor will Mrs Wardle."

Tell that to Barlow, I thought, but had more sense than to say so. I lowered my eyes meekly. "No, Mr Mowbray. Of course not." I waited a moment in case he had more to say, but he only nodded and walked off.

The laundry room *was* hot—that had been no lie—and I was glad when I'd finished. Then it was time for supper before my lady needed to be undressed. Taking it in the housekeeper's room was no fun—I'd much rather have had the chance to get to know the maids working here. Unlike the maids at Marstone Park, they wouldn't resent my position.

Being a proper lady's maid wasn't all good.

. . .

The next morning I got up a little earlier than I needed to, and crept into my lady's dressing room. A housemaid was already there brushing the carpet, a bucket with her dusting cloths standing ready. She had a round face and black hair, and a cheery smile in spite of the early hour.

"Miss Simons!" She bobbed a curtsey, her voice quiet. "Is somethin' wrong?"

"No, not at all."

She shrugged and finished sweeping. When she picked up a dusting cloth, I did too. "I wanted… I mean, I am used to eating with the other servants at Marstone Park." I began to rub the mirror, so as not to delay her in her work. "I've not been a lady's maid long, and Tamworth is teaching me how to go on."

"I heard that." She smiled, and began to polish the clothes press. "My name's Sally. Missin' the gossip, are you?"

"A little."

"Don't blame you. Wardle's above talkin' to the maids." She put a hand on her mouth to stifle a giggle. "I probably shouldn't have said that."

"Are you one of the people left here on board wages?"

"I am that. It's nice to see some life in the place. Things are a bit too quiet when there's no family here. Wardle keeps herself to herself most of the time, and Mowbray's only after a quiet life. It'll be a shock for him, havin' to bestir himself with a full house. Might have to leave the master's port alone."

Port? That might explain the sweet smell on his breath last night. I wondered who else knew—he'd be lucky to escape being arrested for theft if his lordship found out.

"There's only a handful of us normally here," Sally went on. "But they've taken on a few more now the house is opened up. O'Connor's friendly enough—too old for flirtin' with, though. He's the permanent footman." That must be the older man I'd seen with the butler when we arrived yesterday.

By now Sally had dusted the chair and the windows. My lady's dressing table was in her bedroom, so that would have to wait until later, when Sally did the bed.

"Lady Cerney's room next," Sally said, collecting up her tools and letting herself out into the corridor. Feeling I'd made a good start on getting to know the others, I took out a clean chemise and pair of stockings and laid them across the chair, then went down to fetch my lady's hot water.

We set out for Madame Donnard's establishment as soon as their ladyships had finished breakfast. Sitting in the carriage with the two ladies, I did my best not to gawp at all the people in the streets outside, or even peer out of the window.

It wasn't a long journey. Barlow, who'd been riding up behind, went to knock on a red door, smart with shiny paint and brass fittings, before handing the ladies down. By then a young maid had opened the door, and we were shown into a salon furnished with several sofas, a low table, and a couple of cabinets full of dolls dressed in colourful gowns of different styles. I'd have loved to examine them, but I was here to learn what went on at a fashionable mantua-maker, so I stood against the wall and tried to look inconspicuous.

Madame was dressed smartly, looking like a fancier version of a housekeeper in a gown plain enough to show she knew her station, but made from an elegant silver-grey fabric that shone gently where it caught the light. That wasn't the kind of gown us lower sorts might wear. She was old enough to be my mother, but sour-faced where Ma looked cheerful. I was glad I didn't have to work for her.

"Welcome, Lady Cerney—a whole new wardrobe for your niece, your note said?"

Lady Cerney inclined her head, and took a seat while Madame Donnard gushed about how lovely it was to see her ladyship in such good looks. Then Madame turned her attention to Lady Isabella, asking her to stand in the middle of the room. Madame walked around my lady as if she was a sergeant inspecting a recruit, wearing a face that looked like she'd sucked a lemon. And she talked about Lady

Isabella to Lady Cerney as if my lady was deaf or stupid. My lady's lips were pressed together, but she didn't protest.

Two of Madame's assistants came into the room and stood beside me, waiting for orders. They were dressed in some drab fabric, nothing like the gown Madame wore. One of them was told to fetch a partially completed gown that could be fitted quickly. Madame sent Lady Isabella off to be measured by the other assistant, and I trailed behind. Fletcher, this one was called, and she had the thin face and shadowed eyes of illness. Or perhaps she didn't get enough to eat—both, possibly, along with the worry that went with all that. Her looks reminded me of the labourers' wives in the village—the ones where their menfolk drank most of their wages and didn't set enough by for the winter, or the ones with too many mouths to feed and husbands who kept them breeding more.

"I need to measure you with only your chemise and stays on, my lady," Fletcher said. Lady Isabella sighed, but stood with her arms out so Fletcher and I could unpin and unlace. Then Fletcher measured her, making lots of marks on a long strip of paper.

Dawkins, the other assistant, brought in an armful of orange brocade, with patterns of leaves and flowers embroidered on it. Fletcher looked at the gown as Dawkins held it up, then back at Lady Isabella. "Is that the only one we have?"

"The only one far enough along to be ready for tomorrow."

"What's wrong with it?" Lady Isabella asked

Fletcher began to explain, but Dawkins jabbed an elbow in her ribs and interrupted. "Madame will advise you on patterns and styles, my lady. Please, would you try this on so we can see how well it fits?"

It seemed that Madame didn't want anyone else having a different opinion from her. Lady Isabella wasn't pleased with that, and she was even less happy when they dressed her. The gown had a polonaise overskirt, puffed out around her hips and behind, and huge bows of fabric on the stomacher.

"I look as broad as I am high," she said, and she was right.

"You look lovely, my lady," I said. It would be bad enough looking like a decorated orange, without her thinking that she looked ridiculous as well. But I didn't convince her.

"Miss Fletcher, can anything be done to make me seem less... wide?" she said. "*I* can suggest a change to Madame, if I know what to say."

That was clever—but then I'd never thought she was stupid. My lady was just ignorant, and not by her own choice. She'd seen hardly anything of the world beyond Marstone Park.

I listened carefully while Fletcher explained ways the gown could be quickly modified, but Dawkins cut her off before she'd finished, saying they didn't want Madame coming to find out what had taken them so long.

Back in the salon, Madame gushed about how lovely Lady Isabella looked, but Lady Cerney wasn't fooled. Once she threatened to take her business elsewhere—and no mantua-maker would turn down the size of order that Lady Cerney was intending to make—Madame agreed to make some changes. Fletcher brought out some fabrics for a new petticoat; darker colours, and in contrasting shades to distract from the width of the skirts. Lady Isabella duly chose the colour that Fletcher had recommended earlier, and Madame promised that Fletcher would bring the altered gown to Marstone House later that afternoon for a final fitting.

Madame brought out some of the dolls from the cabinet for Lady Cerney to choose from—but all in styles very like the orange one that had not suited my lady and wouldn't do at all. Lady Isabella managed that, too. We were to take some dolls and fabrics away and choose this evening. I guessed she wanted to think about them without being hurried by Madame or Lady Cerney. That left us the rest of the afternoon for shopping.

Barlow was waiting outside the mantua-maker's door—I really wished Mowbray had sent Jem or O'Connor instead.

"You're to take these back to Marstone House." I held out the box with the dolls and fabric samples.

He put his hands behind his back. "I don't take orders from you, Molly Simons."

I sighed. "Lady Cerney's orders."

He thrust his face towards mine. "I saw you sneaking out last night with Langton. What's Jem got that I haven't?"

Manners?

"What I do is none of your business." I held the box out again. "Are you going to take this or not?"

I couldn't have arranged better timing if I'd tried—Lady Cerney came out of the door while Barlow still had his hands behind his back. "Why are you still here? Barlow, isn't it?"

Barlow straightened up, then gave a servile bow.

"Meet us in Bond Street," Lady Cerney instructed. "We'll be in Madame Rousseau's hat shop, or thereabouts."

"Yes, my lady." Barlow snatched the box from my hands and hurried off. If he hadn't been my enemy before, he was now.

CHAPTER 5

Bond Street wasn't far, although it took us a long time to get there. It wasn't only the number of people in the streets, but Lady Cerney's slow pace. There was plenty to see, though, and it was easier to see it on foot than it had been from the carriage. Hawkers sold all manner of things—hot pies, cherries in paper cones, sweetmeats and little cakes, ribbons and bows and pins. I had coins from Mr Archer's purse in my pocket, and if the money had been mine to spend it would have gone long before we reached the hat shop. I had to watch my feet, though—there were horses aplenty. Ragged boys, and some girls, wielded brooms for a penny to clear the street for fine ladies and gentlemen to cross. And for me, following close behind my lady.

The hat shop had a splendid display in the window, different from the few shops in Over Minster. Some of the ones at home had proper displays of all their goods, while others only bothered to put a few things in the window, as the village people knew where to go for what they wanted.

Madame Rousseau's shop window had only one item. It was a hat. Well, obviously it would be—but such a hat! A polished wooden stand shaped like a head was topped by a huge powdered wig, dressed almost as high as Lady Cerney's hair. The wide-brimmed hat perched on top of that was trimmed with ribbons, lace, and tall feathers. And instead of being able to look past the hat into the shop, the whole window behind it was draped in a fine muslin that must have cost a pretty penny.

"Never seen a hat before?" Barlow asked, making me jump as he spoke behind me. The ladies had already gone into the shop. It hadn't taken him long to take the box and return—not long enough for me, certainly. I made to enter the shop, but he leaned with one hand against the door frame, blocking my way.

"You're getting above yourself, Moll. Just 'cause you dine with the housekeeper now, doesn't mean you're any better than the rest of us."

I put my hands on my hips. "Funny how sitting higher up the servants' table used to make you better than me. It's a different story now, isn't it?"

He scowled, but didn't move.

"Get out of my way, Barlow. My mistress is expecting me inside."

He moved his arm, slowly, and took a step back so I either had to go around him or squeeze between him and the wall. I went around, but he still reached out and patted my bottom as I passed him. I hardly felt it through all the layers of skirt and petticoat, but that wasn't the point. He was going to be real trouble, was Barlow.

Lady Cerney looked around as I entered, but turned her attention back to a wall display with more fancy hats. "That would do nicely for you, Isabella." She pointed at one with tall, fluffy feathers in it.

"Those feathers are nearly as tall as me!" Lady Isabella exaggerated a bit, but not much. The shop assistant wasn't like Madame Donnard—she didn't try to persuade the ladies that she knew better. Instead, she showed them a different hat, made in a dark blue that brought out the colour of Lady Isabella's eyes, and with a more modest plume. Well, I say more modest, but it still looked huge to me. It was more in proportion, though, and my lady put it on and admired herself in the large mirror on one wall. She looked like she was enjoying herself, and no wonder—she'd never had so many fine clothes and things in her life, even though Lord Marstone was rich.

"We'll take both of those," Lady Cerney said. "The first will do nicely for me. Now, show me some headdresses suitable for evening wear."

"These all look very expensive, Aunt," Lady Isabella said, as the assistant put the hats into boxes and brought out more creations in all sorts of colours and styles.

"Madame Rousseau makes the best hats, Isabella. She is one of the most expensive, true, but quality has to be paid for."

"Doesn't my father mind spending all this money?"

Lady Cerney hmpfed. "He won't find out until they send the bills, then he'll have no choice."

"He'll find out sooner than that," I muttered, but I must have said it louder than I thought.

"What do you mean, girl?" Lady Cerney's voice was sharp.

"Sorry, my lady. I spoke out of turn." I had to learn to keep my mouth shut—I couldn't spoil my chances on my first day in London.

"How will Marstone find out?" Lady Cerney asked, keeping her voice down this time.

"My lady, Barlow'll know which shops you go into, and have a good idea of how much you've bought if he has to carry it all back."

"Does he report to Lord Marstone?"

I was tempted to say yes, but that would have been a lie. "I don't know for sure, my lady. But he does like getting other people into trouble when he can."

Lady Cerney nodded, and I let out a breath of relief as she turned her attention to the row of headdresses now on the counter. Lovely, they were, in all colours—silk, some of them, by the sheen—and adorned with bows and frills, feathers and ribbons, and even artificial flowers and fruits. I didn't learn nearly as much here as I had listening to Fletcher at the mantua-makers though—mostly what I found out was that Lady Cerney had no idea how to choose things that would suit Lady Isabella.

"Have those delivered to Marstone House," Lady Cerney finally said. Seven hat boxes stood on the counter, and although they weren't heavy, they were big. Even Barlow and Jem between them might have trouble managing all those.

That gave me an idea.

Gloves were next, only a few doors further along the street. Long, white gloves—for balls, Lady Cerney said—and wrist-length ones in buttery-soft leather. And each pair costing enough to feed a village family for weeks. Then dancing shoes, and half-boots for walking or carriage rides.

"I'll give those to Barlow to take back, my lady," I offered, when they'd tired of emptying the shoe shop. Some were being made for them and would be delivered later, but four boxes with ready-made shoes stood on the counter. The shopkeeper could well have delivered the whole lot, but Lady Cerney didn't object, so I took the boxes out and gave them to Barlow—with his arms full, he couldn't slap my bum again.

The ladies vanished into another shop—undergarments, I thought—but I didn't follow them right away. Barlow disappeared into the crowds and I looked around. Finally, I spotted what I was looking for—a young lad with a broom, waiting to sweep a crossing. He was skinny, with a grubby face and tattered clothes, and he was paying as much attention to a pieman as to possible customers. He'd do.

"One, please," I said to the pieman, and handed over some pennies. Then I stood back against the wall and beckoned the boy over. Close-to, I reckoned he was older than he looked, just small—from lack of food, most likely.

"Want this?"

He narrowed his eyes—rightly suspecting it wasn't going to be a gift. "What d'yer want?"

"Did you see the footman I just gave some boxes to?"

"Yeah." I gave him the pie, but he didn't eat.

"He'll be back, and later on he'll have a lot more parcels. Do you think you can trip him up so he drops them all?"

"Yeah." He took a bite of the pie.

"Don't steal any of them, mind—it's not worth getting hanged for. Just trip him and run away."

He shook his head, mouth too full to speak.

"There'll be a penny or two for you afterwards. We'll be around here for a while—don't let him spot you."

He nodded.

"My name's Molly Simons. What's yours?"

I could tell he didn't want to part with that information, and I wasn't going to insist. I didn't really need to know. But he muttered, "Sprout."

It must be a nickname. No parson would christen a baby that, but who's to say he'd even been christened at all?

"Do we have an agreement, Sprout?"

"Yes, miss." He didn't look too happy about it, but he did follow as I went back to the ladies.

The undergarment shop was ideal. Lady Cerney seemed to be buying herself a whole new wardrobe as well as outfitting Lady Isabella properly. One assistant brought chemises and stockings and fichus out for Lady Cerney's inspection; another was kept busy wrapping each item in silver paper, then bundling them into larger parcels wrapped in brown paper and string. By the time she'd done four parcels, the green of Barlow's coat was visible through the window.

"I'll give these to the footman." I picked up the parcels. Once I handed them over I told Barlow to wait, then brought out some wrapped chemises that I'd got to before the assistant parcelled them up. I balanced them on top of the pile, ignoring Barlow's protest and telling him to take them to Marstone House. Then I hurried back into the shop—I didn't want to be too close to the mishap.

Sprout must have done what I asked, for Barlow's shouted curses were loud enough to attract Lady Cerney's attention, and she went to the door.

"It's your chemises, all over the road, my lady!" I tried to sound surprised as I looked out of the window, but she didn't take any notice as she strode out to see what the disturbance was. Lady Isabella looked at me, one brow raised a little. I thought she was about to ask me what had happened, but then she whispered, "Tell me later." She caught on quickly.

When I stepped out of the shop, Barlow was getting to his feet, brushing dirt from the knees of his fancy breeches and looking very silly with his wig askew. I'd have been satisfied with that, but Barlow made it worse for himself.

"Pick up the parcels before they get stolen," Lady Cerney ordered.

Barlow saw me behind Lady Cerney—and I didn't try to hide my smug expression. He jabbed an angry finger in my direction. "It's her fault, my lady. Don't blame me for this."

That was his big mistake. Lady Cerney stiffened. "You appear to be telling me what to do. Did I mishear?"

She was good—very good. He couldn't agree without telling her she was mistaken, or disagree without admitting his insolence. He looked at the ground, shuffling his feet.

"Blaming others for your own mistakes is not an attribute I appreciate in my staff," she went on, in a voice that could have frozen flames. "Simons was in the shop with me when you dropped my purchases. And you have yet to pick them up."

Barlow began to gather the parcels, but by now there weren't quite as many chemises as there should have been. I hadn't seen Sprout when I came out of the shop, but there were enough others around who would have taken advantage.

"Take them back to Marstone House, and send someone else. That other footman who came with us from Marstone Park—he'll do." She turned to me as Barlow continued to scrabble on the ground. "Simons, go back into the shop and order another set of chemises, then wait for the other man. There is a perfumer's shop further down the road; you will find us there." She swept off, Lady Isabella following with a grin over her shoulder for me.

Barlow would try to get back at me later, no doubt, but at least I wouldn't have to fend off his wandering hands for the rest of the day.

I watched as he stalked away down the street. There was a quiet cough beside me—Sprout hadn't wasted any time coming for his payment. He seemed happy with the few pennies I gave him, and winked at me as he went off to lurk by a busy shop doorway, waiting for someone who'd pay to have the horse droppings and other muck swept from their path.

Jem dropped the parcels he was carrying on my lady's bed, and deposited a sealed letter on top of them, wearing the same frown he'd had all afternoon—when their ladyships weren't looking. He had too much sense to show any feeling in front of his employer's family.

"What's wrong?" I stood by the bedchamber door, blocking Jem's way out. He might not have taken the same fancy to me as I had to him, but he'd always been polite and I didn't think he'd push me out of the way.

"You, that's what's wrong. Barlow could lose his position because of you."

Me? "He did that to himself—I didn't make him answer back to Lady Cerney."

Jem's expression didn't change. "He wouldn't have dropped the parcels if you hadn't piled them so high."

It sounded like Barlow hadn't realised how he'd come to trip. That was good—I didn't want him keeping a lookout for Sprout next time he was in that area. Although the chances of him accompanying Lady Cerney must be small now.

Jem was still berating me. "Just because he's taken a fancy to Sally, there's no need for—"

"You think I'm jealous?" Over *Barlow*?

"Why else would you do something like that? You've no need, you're—" He shook his head. "Bloody women are nothing but trouble." He muttered the last words, but I heard them clearly enough.

I opened my mouth to explain, but thought better of it. He'd already made up his mind, it seemed, and my temper got the better of me. "My fault, is it? Barlow speaks as he shouldn't to Lady Cerney, and it's *my* fault?" My voice was getting louder, and that would never do, so I stalked off into the dressing room, slamming the door behind me. Silly, really—it wouldn't improve his impression of me.

Not that I should care.

I went to look out of the window. I *had* set up the situation that got Barlow into trouble, but Jem Langton didn't know that. And if Barlow had apologised to Lady Cerney and picked up the parcels, nothing would have come of it.

If Barlow really had taken a fancy to Sally, I should ask her about it. She might enjoy his attentions—tastes differ, after all. But she might not.

I shouldn't have ripped up at Langton like that, either. It wouldn't help my lady if the two people looking out for her were at odds with each other.

Men! More bother than they were worth.

CHAPTER 6

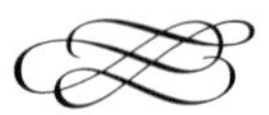

I went back into Lady Isabella's bedroom as soon I was sure Langton had gone. The letter he'd left was addressed to my lady, so I put it in my pocket before anyone else could come into the room and see it.

My lady would be coming upstairs soon, so I piled all the packages in the dressing room and went to the kitchens to order a tea tray. By the time I returned, she had arrived and had the fashion dolls spread out on her bed, examining them with a little frown on her face.

I put the tray on the table by the window, and took out the letter. "Langton gave me this, my lady."

She broke the seal and read it while I poured her cup of tea. She frowned, so it wasn't good news. "Molly, the letter says that you know Archer."

"Yes, my lady. I spoke to him last night. He asked me to tell him where you would be each day, if possible, so Mr Carterton can meet you."

She nodded at that, but her frown hadn't gone. "It seems you and Langton know more about this than I do."

"Sorry, my lady. Mr Archer said as how Lord Wingrave would explain it in his letter."

She sighed, then shrugged and went over to her bed. "Never mind. Now, come and look at these dolls with me."

Between us, we chose some that we thought might suit, but I didn't think the dolls were very helpful. They were about a foot tall with their clothes made from the same fabrics as the full size gowns, but what draped well on a grown woman stuck out stiffly on the dolls. They were better than nothing, though, and we picked a few that didn't have obviously wide skirts.

Things went better later that afternoon, when Fletcher came with the orange gown and its new, dark petticoat. She had Lady Isabella stand on a stool while she adjusted the pins in the hem, and my lady asked if Fletcher had time to give her some advice about the dolls.

"I'm expected back, my lady," Fletcher said, with an anxious look at the clock. If I worked for Madame Donnard, I wouldn't want to risk angering her, either.

"Madame will be angry if you delay, I suppose." Lady Isabella looked disappointed. I didn't blame her. Fletcher—and maybe that Dawkins—seemed to be the only people who had any idea how to choose styles and colours for her.

"It's a pity my lady was busy when you arrived, Miss Fletcher," I suggested. "You had to wait half an hour to do the fitting."

Fletcher was too honest for her own good, for it took her a moment to work out what I meant. "I… I could say that."

"I'll make it worth your while," my lady said. Fletcher nodded, and carried on with her adjustments. When she'd finished, Lady Isabella sent her to look at the dolls and fabrics while I unpinned the gown. Even then, my lady had to promise that Madame would not find out Fletcher had advised her.

By the time I'd put my lady back into her day gown, Fletcher had sorted through the dolls and samples, and I listened carefully while she explained why some styles and fabrics would suit and some would not.

Lady Isabella gave her some coin at the end of it all, and I escorted

Fletcher downstairs while my lady sat down with pen and paper to make a note of what she wanted to order when she returned to the mantua-maker.

I asked Fletcher to wait in the back entrance, and went to the kitchen to beg some of that morning's left over bread rolls and a lump of cheese. I did wonder if I would offend her, but I needn't have worried—she was grateful for even that little extra.

I hoped the seamstress Ma had worked for hadn't been as dreadful as Madame. It made me even more determined not to lose my present position.

Not a lot happened the next day—not to me, that is. Lady Isabella had her first dancing lesson. I'd have loved to watch, but I was kept busy ironing her new chemises and storing everything away so it wouldn't crease—all under Tamworth's close supervision. There was a woman who came in to do the laundry, but Tamworth insisted that I needed to know how to do these things myself if I was to ensure my lady's clothing was kept properly. O'Connor walked past the open door during one of Tamworth's lectures, and gave me a sympathetic grin and a wink. I was hard put to keep my face straight.

By the time my lady's dancing lesson was over, the finished orange gown had arrived from Madame Donnard. Lady Cerney was to take Lady Isabella to Madame Donnard's to order more gowns, and then to calls on other fine ladies. I helped my lady into the new gown, and Tamworth showed me how to do up her hair in a fancier style—all powdered and padded high. I wondered if she was trying to make Lady Isabella look taller, which it did, but I thought it gave her head an unbalanced look. And old, with the grey powder. Even with Fletcher's adjustments I couldn't truthfully say my lady looked good in the orange gown, either. She thought the same, I'm sure, for she didn't set out with the air of someone looking forward to meeting people.

The next day they went off to look at some paintings, and she looked a little happier when she came back from that. She was still in the orange gown, so I wondered what had improved her confidence. Perhaps she found it easier not having to talk to too many people?

Tamworth spent most of that day lecturing me again, this time about face paints and powders, and receipts to cure freckles, spots on the face and the like. She gave me a little notebook so I could write down things I needed to remember. I started to make notes, but when Tamworth saw what I'd put I got a strict talking-to about improving my writing and spelling. It seemed a proper lady's maid needed more skills with words than the village school had managed to put into me. I don't know how she expected me to learn, though, with no teacher.

Fletcher returned on the second afternoon, to fit some of Lady Isabella's new gowns. She pinned the hems and made some bodice adjustments to a blue walking dress, and my lady tried to find out how she knew so much about styles and fashions. All Fletcher would say was that she used to be a lady's maid.

When she'd finished pinning, I offered to sew the hems so she could get on with fitting the ball gown she'd brought with her. I was only meaning to be helpful, but there were even more worry lines on her face than before as she looked at Lady Isabella. "I'm sorry, my lady, but I can't complete the ball gown this evening."

My lady smiled—she was always kind to the people who worked for her. "Don't worry, Fletcher, I'm not expecting you to. You said you were a lady's maid once—does that mean you know about hair styles?"

"Yes, my lady."

"When you have finished pinning the ball gown, and if Madame is not expecting you to go back to her salon this evening, I would like you to show Molly how to arrange my hair in a way that suits me."

"She is not expecting me, my lady, but I have—"

"I will pay you for your time."

Fletcher sighed. "It's not that, my lady. I have to… that is, Billy…"

My lady said she would get a message taken, but Fletcher didn't want to write a note. I went to fetch Langton while Fletcher pinned the ballgown. He couldn't ignore a request from my lady, but he scowled as he followed me upstairs. Obviously one to bear a grudge.

Fletcher asked Langton to tell someone called Ruby that she'd be a couple of hours late, and could she see to Billy. After what Tamworth had said that day, I wondered if it was this Ruby who could not read, rather than Fletcher not being able to write.

Who was Billy, and who was Ruby? Did Fletcher have another job in the evenings—cooking for this Billy, perhaps, and Ruby was another servant there who could do it for her this once? As if it wasn't bad enough being overworked by Madame Donnard.

And Langton grimaced when Fletcher told him where to take the message. I thought for a moment he was going to protest, but he finally nodded, repeated the message back, and left.

Never mind learning to read and write better—I had quite enough to learn from Fletcher about hair. Lady Isabella was very patient, sitting quietly in front of her mirror while Fletcher showed me how to put her hair up in different arrangements, make long curls that draped over her shoulder, and use the curling irons to make tight ringlets that would stay in for a whole day. It felt far more useful than the things Tamworth was teaching me.

By the time Fletcher left it was quite late, but she had taken away a handful of coins, and I'd scrounged a bit more food from Cook for her.

Lady Isabella met Mr Carterton the next afternoon. He was to go to the park with my lady and Lady Cerney in the Marstone calèche, and I found an excuse to be on the stairs when he arrived and was shown into the front parlour. He was slim, not much older than Langton, with dark blond hair tied back without powder, and he dressed very plain. Langton looked much finer, with his broad shoulders in his laced coat and his wig.

My lady was looking very well, dressed in her new walking gown and the blue hat. I'd managed to do her hair nicely, I thought—not near so high as the day before, unpowdered, and all over loose curls beneath the hat's broad brim. Tamworth had tutted, but had to agree that what suited her own mistress did not suit mine.

When Lady Cerney was eventually ready, Mr Carterton offered

his arm and the three of them walked down the steps to the calèche. Langton climbed onto the step behind, and they set off.

Tamworth descended the stairs behind me as Mowbray closed the front door. I was expecting more instruction, but she merely told me to occupy myself pressing Lady Isabella's new fichus, as the laundry-woman couldn't be trusted with them. Then she headed for the baize door—for tea with Mrs Wardle, I suspected. Funny, wasn't it, how the laundrywoman was good enough to deal with Lady Cerney's things, which were just as fine? But there was nothing to be done about it, so I put the irons to heat and went to collect the fichus.

Sally came by while I was busy with the irons, and leaned over to finger the delicate fabric. "Lovely, that is."

I hoped she had time to talk for a while, without neglecting her duties, but that hope only lasted a few seconds.

"Simons!"

We both started and turned to the door. It was Barlow, a smug grin on his face. "Mrs Wardle wants to see you in her room. Now."

Sally rolled her eyes, and took herself off. I couldn't see anything in her expression that said she'd taken a fancy to Barlow.

I put the iron aside, wondering what this was about—Barlow clearly thought I was in trouble. I didn't answer to the housekeeper, but it wouldn't do to ignore such a summons, so I walked over to the door, stopping before I reached it.

Barlow glared at me. "Now, she said. What are you waiting for?"

"You to get out of my way. If you think I'm going to give you another chance to grope me, you can think again."

He folded his arms. "And what if I won't move?"

"Then I'll explain to Mrs Wardle why it took me so long to get to her room. And to Lady Cerney and Lady Isabella."

Barlow scowled, but finally stood back.

"After you," I said, not moving. He swore, and stamped off along the hallway. I gave him a few seconds and followed. He loitered by the housekeeper's door as I knocked and heard her reply.

"Shut the door, Simons," Mrs Wardle said, from her chair by the fire. "No need for Barlow to overhear," she added more quietly. "Sit down." She didn't look angry, but she didn't look particularly friendly, either. "Barlow says he saw you take food from the kitchen yesterday. Cook has not complained, so you cannot have stolen much, but it is the principle that—"

"I didn't steal anything," I interrupted, indignation getting the better of my manners. "I'm sorry, Mrs Wardle, I shouldn't have spoken while you were talking. But I asked Cook, and she said I could take some leftover bread and cheese."

Her brows rose. "Do we not feed you enough?"

I explained about Fletcher, and she began to look more friendly. "We cannot feed everyone, Simons," she said when I had finished. "If Cook agreed, then there is no problem. But why would Barlow seek to cause trouble?"

I wondered if Barlow had said anything about his 'accident' on Bond Street, and felt my face going hot. Luckily for me, Mrs Wardle assumed something else.

"Turned him down, did you?"

I nodded.

"Did you encourage him?"

"No!" That came out too loud. "Not at all."

She shook her head with a sigh. "He was trouble last year, but I have no say in the hiring of footmen. And most of the time Mowbray is too… Well, never mind that."

Wonderful! The two people in charge of the servants couldn't or wouldn't help me if Barlow turned into even more of a problem. I'd have to do my best to stay out of his way.

My lady was in an odd mood when she returned from the drive with Mr Carterton. She appeared happy, but every now and then her face became serious. Thoughtful, perhaps. She went straight up to her room, and I followed to help her off with her redingote and hat.

"Did you enjoy yourself, my lady?" I asked, as I teased out some of the curls that had been crushed by the hat. "Did you feel better in your new clothes?"

She met my eyes in the mirror, and a mischievous smile appeared. "Yes, very much so. I managed to repay some unkind comments made to me about my orange dress."

I didn't know what she was talking about, but I smiled. The new clothes had given her confidence, and rightly so. A small frown reappeared but there was no time for more, as she was to take tea with Lady Cerney.

I escaped to the housemaids' room, where the female servants sat if they had some free time. I had a piece of lace that I pretended to mend while I waited for a chance to ask Langton what had happened that afternoon. He was bound to go past the open door at some time. Sally carried an armful of linens down the corridor, and I heard Barlow's voice. Going to the doorway to look, I saw Sally shrug and walk around Barlow—it seemed she didn't care for him any more than I did. I turned to go back to my mending, only to find Langton standing behind me.

"Still jealous, eh?"

I wasn't going to answer that. "Did anything happen on the drive?" I asked, keeping my voice low so only Langton could hear.

He shrugged. "We drove around. Mr Carterton went for a walk on the grass with Lady Isabella. They got back in."

Well, that was useful! I wouldn't bother asking him in future, not if he was going to be so sulky about it and didn't see anything anyway. I'd do better encouraging my lady to talk.

I whiled away the time a little longer, until it was the hour Fletcher was due to arrive for another fitting. But when the scullery maid led someone in from the area door, it was a woman I'd never seen.

"Where's Fletcher?"

"I'm Nokes. Fletcher couldn't come."

"Why not? Is she ill?" I wouldn't be surprised, the way she'd looked last time she came.

Nokes pressed her lips together and said nothing. I didn't persist, not near the flapping ears of the people going to and fro below stairs.

"You'd best come up then." I put my bit of sewing into a pocket and picked up one of the bags she was carrying. They were large—not heavy, but awkward. By rights, I should have had a footman carry them up, but O'Connor was on front door duty and I was still out of sorts with Langton. And I certainly wasn't going to ask Barlow, so I carried one up myself.

I hoped Fletcher wasn't in some kind of trouble.

CHAPTER 7

The first gown Nokes brought out to be fitted was for evening wear, in lemon and cream stripes. The colours suited my lady much better than the orange gown, and even though it was still only half-sewn, it was clear as we fitted it to her that it would be not near so wide.

Lady Isabella asked why Fletcher had not come. Nokes seemed as if she wasn't going to say anything again, but couldn't refuse to answer a lady. "Fletcher doesn't work for Madame Donnard any more, my lady."

My lady turned to face the seamstress. "She said nothing of leaving when she was here yesterday. What has happened?"

"If you please, my lady, would you stand still while I finish pinning these seams?"

Lady Isabella did as she was asked and Nokes worked on for a bit, but she didn't know how persistent my lady could be. "So why *did* Fletcher leave?"

"Madame said she'd been stealing. Madame said Fletcher should be grateful that she hadn't called the constable."

"Fletcher didn't seem the type of person who'd steal," Lady Isabella said. That was exactly what I'd been thinking.

"It didn't seem right to us, either, my lady. Sarah was good at her job, and kind as well."

"Will she get another position?" Lady Isabella asked.

"I'm sure I couldn't say, my lady."

Not without a character, she wouldn't, and Madame wouldn't be giving her one.

Lady Isabella persisted with her questions, and Nokes told her that Fletcher had been accused of keeping money meant for Madame—most likely the money my lady had given her the day before. What a horrible person Madame must be—Ma hadn't liked the woman she'd worked for in her London days, but she'd never told me of anything like that happening to her. I wondered if Madame was jealous; Fletcher had a better eye for colour and style than she did, that was certain.

"Where does she live, do you know?" Lady Isabella asked. "I mean her no harm, I assure you."

"I don't know, my lady. She kept herself to herself, mostly." I thought Nokes was telling the truth, although she might not have told my lady even if she did know. With an employer like Madame, why would she trust anyone else?

Nokes had finished with that gown, and I helped her take it off, only pricking my fingers on the pins a few times. Nokes folded it up to be taken back to the salon while I helped my lady into the ivory silk ball gown for its final finishing. When Nokes had sewn the last adjustments, and pocketed a shilling from my lady for her efforts, I showed her to the top of the servants' stair.

"Molly, what can I do about Fletcher?" Lady Isabella asked when I returned and started to unfasten the ball gown. "If I hadn't asked her to do extra, she would still have her job."

"It wasn't your fault, my lady. Fletcher didn't have to stay." It wasn't Fletcher's fault either—teaching hair arrangements wasn't part of her job and Madame had no right to expect the money to be given to her.

"I can explain to Madame Donnard."

"It wouldn't help." My lady had no idea how nasty people could be to each other. "Folks like her won't admit to being wrong. I'll bet she gets that shilling off Nokes tomorrow, as well. Besides, you can't do nothing about it, my lady, not if you don't know where she lives."

"But we do! Molly, ask Langton if he can recall where he took the message the other night."

I remembered Langton's face when he'd heard the address. "I can ask, my lady. But I doubt it'll be a place you should go. You'd be robbed, like as not. Or worse." Ma had been very keen on telling me the evils that could befall young women in the wrong parts of London —and even in the right parts, sometimes. She'd been warning me, of course, but she wasn't one to exaggerate, and I thought the dangers would be worse for someone like Lady Isabella in her fine gowns.

"I'll take precautions." My lady had that stubborn look about her—if I didn't ask Langton, she'd ask herself.

"Very well, my lady." But that could wait until tomorrow.

The next day Lady Isabella had her dancing lesson in the morning, went out with Lady Cerney in the afternoon, and went to the theatre in the evening. All I did was have another set of lectures from Tamworth.

"What's the theatre like, my lady?" I asked as I was undressing her that evening. I'd never had to work this late at Marstone Park, but at least no-one could order me around while my lady was out, so I wasn't actually working much longer hours than I used to.

"Oh… Big. Lots of people." She yawned as I began to comb and braid her hair.

I'd guessed that. Maybe one day I'd get to go myself.

"I'm going to a rout tomorrow night," she went on, "and to Vauxhall in five days." She yawned again, and she didn't seem inclined to say more.

It wasn't until I was in my bedroom that I remembered I was supposed to have asked Langton where he'd taken the message for Ruby. But it was too late now. She'd said nothing more about finding Fletcher, and I hoped she'd changed her mind.

. . .

I rose early the next morning, having given some thought to my lady's engagements during the night. Mr Archer wanted to be told, and Langton was the obvious person to take a message. But it was difficult to get him alone, and I didn't want to do that unless there wasn't any other choice, not after the way he'd been acting. Instead, I found the little book and pencil Tamworth had given me and carefully cut out the back page. A rout, and Vauxhall. I had no idea what either of them were, or how to spell them, but I did my best. Slipping the note to Langton would be far easier than telling him, but I was certain my spelling wasn't right, and I wasn't going to give him a chance to laugh at me.

Not that I cared what he thought.

The Dog and Partridge, Mr Archer had said, on Davies Street. I didn't know where that was, and I couldn't ask anyone here without folks wondering why I wanted to know. Maids had no business asking about public houses. But I should be able to remember my way to Bond Street, so I slipped out of the house. The kitchen maid, already busy setting out the servants' breakfast, looked up as I walked past the kitchen then turned back to her work. It was nice not to have to explain myself to anyone.

The streets were quite different from when I'd accompanied the ladies—the rich folk were still in their beds, and I made my way around and between street sellers shouting their wares and women returning with fish from the market or the morning's bread. But the crossing sweepers were out looking for business, all the same. I was trying to find Sprout—as one who'd done as he'd been asked before—but if he wasn't here, I would ask someone for directions to Davies Street.

Sprout found me. He sidled up and asked if I was looking for something in particular.

"The Dog and Partridge. D'you know where that is?"

He nodded eagerly. "I can show yer."

"I need to get back, but I've a note to be delivered. Can you do that?" I showed him some pennies in my hand. "It's to be given to Mr

Archer, who's staying there. Or left for him, if he's not in. He needs to get it this morning."

"Easy, miss. I'll go now."

I dropped a couple of pennies into his hand and gave him the note. He set off up the street, the same way I was going, so I followed him.

He stopped and faced me. "I'll do it, miss, 'onest! I done what yer asked before, din' I?"

"I'm not following you, Sprout. I'm going back to Grosvenor Square."

He stared at me, his expression turning wary.

"What's the matter?"

"Dog an' Partridge is between 'ere an' Grosvenor Square." He clutched the note in his fist. I couldn't work out what was worrying him at first, then I realised.

"You can still take it." I didn't want to go asking for a man in a public house. "But you can show me where it is, in case I ever need to go there myself."

Sprout was happy with that, and weaved his way through the people in the street, turning a couple of corners and stopping outside a respectable-looking place with clean windows and a smell of frying bacon wafting out that made my stomach rumble. I fished out another penny for the lad, and he pointed out the short way to Grosvenor Square.

When I went upstairs after having my breakfast, my lady was still asleep, and in danger of being late for her dancing practice. I hurried her into her gown and did her hair in a simple knot. It wasn't until she returned from her lesson that she told me what she had in mind for that afternoon. I should have known she wouldn't forget about Fletcher.

"Today, my lady?" I asked, dismayed.

"Yes, today. My aunt has gone to a card party, and I said I needed to rest before tonight's rout. I saw Senhor da Gama at the theatre last night, and he is to meet us at two o'clock, on the corner of Green Street and Park Street."

That was an odd name. "A foreign gentleman?"

She nodded, a dreamy smile appearing. "Yes, he's Portuguese. You said it would be a place I shouldn't go alone, Molly, so Senhor da Gama will escort me. I need you and Langton, too."

If I remembered rightly, I'd said it would be somewhere she shouldn't go. At all, I'd meant. But her mouth was set and I didn't think I'd be able to dissuade her. She was like to go off on her own if I wouldn't help. Only Langton knew where to go, but if he refused to say, I wouldn't put it past her to interview all the seamstresses at Madame Donnard's until someone told her where to find Fletcher.

Would she go with only this Senhor da Gama to escort her? That could ruin her reputation. I'd have to try to get Langton on his own after all. Unless…

"Did Lady Cerney take a footman with her? If it was Langton, we can't—"

"No. She said Lady Henderson was to call for her."

That excuse was gone, then. But my lady would only have made another attempt—and this way she didn't need to know that I'd forgotten to ask Langton about Ruby's address.

Langton wasn't the only problem. "You can't go like that, my lady." I waved a hand at her gown. It was plain, compared to her ball gowns, but was still finer than the likes of Fletcher would have. She'd stick out like a sore thumb in the kind of place Fletcher must live.

"Did you bring my disguise from Marstone Park?"

I sighed, and went to unearth it from the bottom of the closet in the dressing room. It would be creased, but that wouldn't matter. As I was unpinning my lady, I turned my mind to how to get out of the house without being seen. Barlow was the main problem—if any of the new maids saw us, they'd be curious, but could probably be bribed to keep quiet with a shilling or two. O'Connor, too. Barlow, though, would delight in catching me doing something I shouldn't, even if Lady Isabella suffered for it as well. In fact, telling on us would probably earn him some kind of reward from Lord Marstone.

When my lady's gown was laced, I left her to stuff her hair into a cap and went back into the dressing room. One of her gowns had knots of red ribbon; I cut off a tiny piece and wrapped it in a screw of tissue paper. I might need an excuse to separate Langton from anyone he was with.

"I'll get Langton, my lady. I'll come and fetch you when he's ready."

Green Street and Park Street, I repeated to myself as I hurried down the service stairs. I didn't know where those roads were, but Langton would.

Langton and O'Connor were lounging in the servants' hall, Langton with a book open in front of him and O'Connor trying to build a tower out of playing cards. Barlow must be on door duty—that made things easier.

"Lady Isabella needs more of this ribbon before this evening." I dropped the little packet on the table in front of O'Connor. "Ten yards, if you please. You're to ask Mowbray for the money."

He stood up, picking up the ribbon and putting it in a pocket. "It's a lovely day outside, so it is. Just the day for a walk."

When O'Connor had gone, Langton looked at me with his eyes narrowed. "Does she really need ribbon?"

I looked around, but there was no-one else within hearing. "She wants to find Miss Fletcher. Wherever it was you took the note a few days ago."

"No. It's too dangerous." He hadn't even paused before replying, which confirmed my feeling that Lady Isabella shouldn't be going there. Nor me, come to that.

I gave him all the reasons we should go that I'd just told myself. "The only way you can be sure to stop her," I finished, "is by telling Lady Cerney what she wants to do. And that's likely to get her taken back to Marstone Park or locked up until her father can personally supervise her doings. Lord Wingrave won't be too pleased about that."

"He'll be even more angry if she comes to harm in St Giles." But his shoulders slumped as if he knew he was on the losing side in the argument.

"What's St Giles? A church?"

"Good grief, no." He took off his wig and ran a hand through his short hair. "It's an area of London. Who's the bloke that's to go with her?"

"Senhor da Gama. I don't know anything about him."

"Two o'clock, you say?" He pulled a watch out. "Fifteen minutes or so." He went quiet for a moment, staring at the ceiling, then nodded.

"Barlow's in the front hall. Best if my lady pretends to walk in the back garden, then you can go out by the gate where we went to meet Archer. I'll find a hackney, and meet you on the corner. Go out of the square on North Audley Street, and turn left when you get to Green Street. Wait at the next junction. Don't go further without me."

He sounded very definite, and I didn't care for being ordered about like that, not by a footman. But he knew London and I did not. "All right."

He ran off up the stairs, leaving me to follow at a more normal pace.

I'd persuaded him, but I really, really wished I'd been able to persuade Lady Isabella *not* to go, instead.

CHAPTER 8

We got out of the garden and the mews without anyone spotting us. It wasn't far to the corner where we were to meet. The man waiting for us had a brownish face, as if he'd been out in the sun too much, and black eyebrows. He looked as fine as a footman in a blue coat with silver braiding that matched the top of his cane, and a snowy white wig beneath a tricorne hat. So much for getting my lady to put her oldest clothes on.

He didn't notice us until Lady Isabella stood right in front of him, then he made a low bow, almost hiding his surprise at the way she was dressed. "My lady, where do you wish to go?"

His voice was smooth and the look in his dark eyes would have melted lead, so I wasn't surprised when my lady blushed and stammered out her request. He didn't appear best pleased to find we were to go in search of a servant—he looked the type to consider the likes of me beneath his notice.

"Anything to please a lady," he said, and made a fancy wave of his hand. My lady giggled, like a silly maid—but then, she knew less of life than most maids, silly or not.

"Molly, where is Langton?"

He'd taken his time getting the hackney, but a tattered carriage drew up beside us as she spoke, and Langton jumped down from beside the driver. He'd changed out of his livery, and looked nearly as scruffy as the driver.

Langton must have gone some way from Grosvenor Square to find a hackney that smelled so bad—like someone had cast up their accounts in it, or been carrying raw fish past their best. Or both. I peered in—someone had made a bit of an attempt to clean up the inside, even if they hadn't got rid of the smell.

Senhor da Gama protested about the state of the vehicle, but my lady surprised me, and him, by insisting that it would have to do, and climbing in without waiting for his assistance. I followed, then the pretty peacock got in, dusting off the seat before putting his bum on it.

Looking out of the window, it was a bit like our journey to London, but in reverse. We left the fine buildings behind, and the houses got smaller and the roads narrower. It took a lot longer than I thought it would.

The carriage stopped and Langton opened the door. "This is as far as the carriage can go, my lady. The next streets are too narrow. I can take a message while you wait here."

But by then Senhor da Gama had handed her out and she looked around. I imagine she'd never seen really poor people before—too thin and too dirty, in ragged clothing. I had, of course, in the village at home, but never so many in one place.

"Langton, did you see Billy when you came before?" Lady Isabella asked.

"No, my lady. There was only a woman and a lot of brats at the address Miss Fletcher gave me. The woman said it'd cost, but she'd see Billy all right this once. It's a few streets away—what do you want me to say?"

"I wish to speak to her myself."

Langton's eyes flicked to me, and I shrugged.

"Are you sure, my lady? It's not a good—"

"Your mistress has decided," Fancy Man said. "She is under my protection."

I looked from him to Langton, who was taller and wider in the shoulders than Fancy Man, and not too full of his own importance either. I knew who I'd rather have for protection, in spite of what he thought of me. But my lady gave a little smile and her cheeks pinked again.

We were about to set off down an alley when the hackney driver demanded his money. Of course the peacock had to argue, and in spite of my nerves I nearly laughed when he had to jump back as the driver spat at him. But it wasn't at all funny when Senhor da Gama threatened the driver with his cane and Langton had to stop him.

"Sir, you will put Lady Isabella in danger. Look around you."

We had an audience. It wasn't the skinny lads nearest that bothered me—they looked like Sprout, on the watch in case a few coins might be forthcoming. But a group of men had come out of an alehouse further down the alley and were looking too interested in us for my liking. What a fool Fancy Man was for trying to start a fight in such a place, where the local folks would side with the driver. And in front of Lady Isabella, too.

My stomach felt as if it was knotted, but one look at my lady's face and I knew we would carry on. What use would any further protest from me be against Fancy Man's promise that he would look after her?

Langton gave the driver a few coins, and promised more if he was still there when we returned. We set off along the narrow street: Langton in front, me walking next to Lady Isabella, and Fancy Man behind us. The urchins followed, inspecting Fancy Man's laced coat and my lady's redingote. There hadn't been much point in wearing her maid's uniform if she was going to put one of her own outer garments on top. It was an old one, but still much finer than anything worn by the people around us.

"What do they want?" my lady asked, tilting her head towards the children.

"Looking at your clothes, like as not, my lady."

"Should I give them some money?"

"No!" I said it firmly enough to stop her reaching for her purse. "No, my lady. Don't let on you've a full purse, for heaven's sake."

"Why n—?"

"There's some as would steal the clothes off your back, never mind taking all your money."

My lady went quiet then, and we walked on. A woman in a doorway made to approach Fancy Man, her low-cut gown with lace trimmings advertising her trade. But she was as thin-faced as the rest, and Senhor da Gama snapped at her, causing her to shrug and back away. My lady looked as we passed her, and I wondered if she understood what the woman had been offering. There might be some awkward questions later.

If there was a later. Lady Isabella's eyes widened and I looked where she was staring. We were being followed—not only by the street children, but two men as well, and I didn't like the look of them. They were scrawny, no match for Langton or even Fancy Man, but they looked determined. And these houses crowding above the street could hold more like them. Their friends, or even just temporary accomplices in search of easy pickings.

"Langton." My lady's voice wavered, and I swallowed hard. "Can we go back?"

Langton looked around, then shook his head. "Best not, my lady. I can try a different way out of this area, if you wish." He sounded awfully calm, but he walked faster, leading the way around several turns, into narrower alleys. Then he slowed, looking about him with a frown.

He'd mistaken the way. The knot in my stomach almost stopped me breathing.

"Those men…" Fancy Man finally had the sense to be concerned as he pointed back the way we had come. The two men were there, and they looked like the cat about to have the cream.

Lady Isabella clutched my hand, and took a couple of steps back. "I'm sorry, Molly," she whispered.

There was a noise like a knife on steel—Fancy Man's stick had a sword inside. He might be some use, after all.

"Keep an eye out the other way, my lady," Langton said, and went to stand next to Senhor da Gama. He had no weapon. For the first time, I hoped a man was good with his fists. "Molly, if you can, you and my lady run past them…"

Four more men came into the alley. I thought we were doomed for a moment, but breathed again as I recognised their leader. "That's Mr Archer, my lady. We'll be safe now."

And we were. The two men following us took one look at the bruisers Mr Archer had with him, and the business-like way they swung their cudgels, and ran off, pushing past them.

"This way, my lady." Mr Archer took Lady Isabella's arm and dragged her back the way we'd come. He really didn't need to—she was happy enough to go with him.

Fancy Man objected, of course, but Langton grabbed his sword arm and told him he was a damned fool, and he finally shut up. I really hoped Lady Isabella hadn't fallen in love with him—she deserved better. This pretty peacock certainly wasn't using whatever brain he had.

Mr Archer hurried us on until we came back to the stinking hackney we'd arrived in, and ordered the driver to take us all to Davies Street. Senhor da Gama argued, but Lady Isabella pleaded with him and he got in, looking like a sulky child.

We got back to the Dog and Partridge in a much shorter time than the journey to St Giles had taken, and all I could think on the way was that Langton must have got a message to Mr Archer.

Langton had known help would come, and he hadn't told me or Lady Isabella. He'd let us fear for our lives without saying anything. I was ready to tell him exactly what I thought of him when we got out of the hackney in front of the pub, but I couldn't. Not with my lady there, and the other two.

Fancy Man nearly made another scene in the street—he wanted

Lady Isabella to be escorted home by a proper gentleman. I forgot some of my anger with Langton in amusement—the foreign peacock *really* didn't like someone of the lower orders being in charge of the situation.

"I need to get back into the house without being seen," my lady explained quietly, and I was pleased to see she hadn't got that dreamy look on her any more. She looked down at his laced coat, and he must have taken her point, for he made a quick bow and left us, saying he hoped to see her again soon.

"I won't accompany you, my lady," Mr Archer said, when Senhor da Gama had gone. "Some of the grooms at Marstone House still know me, and it's best his lordship doesn't get wind that I'm in Town. I will have a couple of my men follow you at a distance, to be sure you return safely."

Lady Isabella thanked him, looking very embarrassed about it.

"Langton. Miss Simons." Mr Archer stepped closer, and spoke low, so my lady could not hear. "Lord Wingrave's promise to employ you if you lose your positions for helping Lady Isabella does not include helping her to put herself in danger again. Is that clear?"

"She won't, sir," I said. "She was frightened in those streets, and I don't think she'd want to put me into danger again. Or Langton."

"Very well." He gave us a friendly nod and went into the pub.

"This way, my lady." I knew the way back from that morning, and I'd set off next to her when Langton put a hand on my arm.

"Molly, I need to speak to you."

Good. I needed to speak to him, too. Lady Isabella had heard, and gave me a little nod, so I dropped a few paces behind with Langton. As was only proper, I suppose, for a lady with her maid and footman, even if we didn't look our parts.

"How did Mr Archer know where we were?" It's not easy to sound angry when you have to keep your voice low, but I must have managed it. Langton looked surprised.

"I sent a message, and made the hackney driver take a long route to give Archer time to find us." He scowled. "No thanks from you, then?"

"Why didn't you *tell* us? I thought we were going to be killed." Or raped. Or both. "My lady was terrified, too."

"Perhaps that'll teach her to listen to those who know better."

That was insolent—or would be, if he'd said it to Lady Isabella. The trouble was, I agreed with him, which rather took the wind out of my sails. "Why didn't you say something?"

"I didn't know if Archer would arrive in time," he admitted. "And if my lady knew that he was coming, she might have gone anyway before he arrived, so he couldn't try to stop her. And because she knew she'd be safe."

I thought about it for a moment, but had to admit he had a point. "All right then. Thank you, Jem."

"I'm sorry you were frightened." He sounded grudging, but it *was* an apology.

"I did try to persuade her not to, but I didn't know what it would be like—how bad it would be. I've never seen a place like that before."

He shrugged, and I wondered if he was remembering Barlow's comment about me not being any use in London. Then I wondered how *he* seemed to know about the really poor parts of the city. I'd never thought about where he'd grown up. The way he talked sounded a little like the way the people talked around here—but only a little, as if he'd tried to improve his speech.

"...send for him if she plans to do anything similar."

I'd not been paying attention—Mr Archer, he must have meant. "Are we in trouble for going this time?"

He shook his head. "No. I told him what you said, about my lady going on her own if we wouldn't. Although she'd have had that Portuguese with her, I suppose, but he's no more use than a glass hammer."

I sniggered—that was something else we agreed on. Only two things, to be sure. I still resented the way he'd believed Barlow's tale of my jealousy, but this might be a start towards mending things between us.

. . .

By the time I'd got Lady Isabella up to her room unseen, fetched hot water, and left her in a robe while I collected a tea tray, I'd missed tea in the servants' hall as well as my dinner. And my stomach was telling me so, loudly. I left my lady resting and went in search of something to tide me over until supper.

My lady was quiet when I dressed her for the evening's rout, not saying much more than approving the way I did her hair, and giving another apology for the afternoon's events. It didn't seem the time to drop a hint about servants' meal times.

She was even quieter when she returned home later, if that was possible. But the next morning she was already awake when I took her chocolate and hot water up, writing at the little table in her nightgown and robe. When I returned after my breakfast she was still there, staring at the wall and with little more written than when I'd left her.

"You'll be late for breakfast, my lady. And your dancing practice." I went through into the dressing room and took out the same gown she wore every morning.

"I need to finish this, Molly. I won't be long."

As I laid out the gown on her bed, with a clean chemise and stockings, she folded the paper and dropped a blob of wax on it, then handed it to me.

"This is to go to Mr Carterton, Molly, but my aunt mustn't know. Can you give it to Langton?"

"I... yes, my lady." Langton was on door duty—which was a good excuse not to have to speak to him. I could take it to the Dog and Partridge myself now I knew where it was. Mr Archer would see it delivered.

"I want it to go now, Molly. I'll start dressing; you come back up when you've sent it."

"Yes, my lady." At least I'd had my breakfast today, before having to deal with one of her impulses.

When I got to the top of the area steps, Sprout was only a few yards away, waiting with his broom. "Mornin', Miss Simons."

"What are you doing here? Won't you get more business in the shopping streets?" I walked on, not having time to waste, but he trotted along beside me, my legs being rather longer than his.

He shrugged. "I'm doin' better 'ere. That footman give me a shillin' to take a note yesterday. Not the one... yer know."

That must have been the note to Mr Archer. It seemed Sprout could be relied on. But a whole shilling? And me without my little purse.

"I haven't got a shilling on me."

"Yer can pay me later."

"You can have *sixpence* later." We were halfway to Davies Street by now, so even that was a lot for such a short errand. I suppose Langton must have given him more to make sure he took the message.

"All right." He gave a cheeky grin, and I wondered how much Langton had really given him. But I had money from Mr Archer for exactly this kind of thing, and it was no skin off my nose if Sprout gained from it.

I held out the letter. "This is for a gent called Mr Carterton. I don't know where he lives, but Mr Archer does. Can you remember that?"

"Mr Carterton," he repeated, taking the note from my hand and running off, broom trailing behind him.

Mr Carterton called that afternoon to take my lady driving in the park. Tamworth came to get me after Lady Isabella left but, to my surprise, she didn't have any more lectures. Instead, I sat with her in Lady Cerney's dressing room and read a book she gave me while she sewed. It was only a children's story, and of the improving sort that preaches about the rewards of good behaviour, but it was good of her to help me with my reading. I was pleased to find there weren't too many words I couldn't make out, and when it was time to go for our tea, she said she'd find something harder next time.

"It's very kind of you to help me like this."

She patted my shoulder as we entered the housekeeper's room.

"It's no trouble. And it makes a nice change to have someone new to talk to."

I was feeling quite content when Lady Isabella returned—Tamworth was being friendly, I'd had all my meals on time, and my lady would not be getting any more idiotic ideas.

Or so I thought.

CHAPTER 9

The next afternoon we went to St Giles again.

This wasn't such a foolish trip as the last one—Lady Isabella had assured us that Mr Carterton and Mr Archer would be in charge this time, and we were to meet them at Lady Tregarth's house. According to my lady, Lord Wingrave and Lady Tregarth's son were good friends.

Lady Cerney was at another card party so we left by the front door, both of us in our normal clothes. Langton waited for us outside, without his livery, and we walked the short distance. I'd made sure to have something to eat before we set out .

"Come upstairs with me," Lady Tregarth said to Lady Isabella, when the butler admitted us, then looked at me. "You, too...?"

I curtseyed as well as I could with the bag containing our old clothes in my hand. "Molly Simons, my lady."

Lady Tregarth seemed like a kind woman. She took us into her bedroom—at least, I guessed it was from the bottles and brushes on a dressing table. Lady Isabella explained what we were about, and Lady Tregarth sighed. "I suppose you will not be dissuaded; you appear to be as headstrong as your brother."

I bit my lips against a giggle.

"And you, Molly?" Lady Tregarth was looking at me. "Are you sure you want to do this?"

No—but I couldn't say that. "Mr Carterton and Mr Archer will keep us safe, my lady. I'll do exactly what they say."

She asked me to fetch a bag from her dressing room, and at her nod I pulled out the clothing inside. The garments weren't actually damp, but they smelled like it, and a few bits of dirt floated down as I shook out a tattered brown skirt and bodice. They looked to be about the right size for my lady; there was another set that would do for me, and a couple of grubby mob caps. They'd make a better disguise than the clothing I'd brought. When we'd changed, Lady Tregarth made us dirty our hands, rubbing dried soil in well then adding the finishing touches to our skirts by rubbing the loose bits on them. Lady Tregarth's upstairs maid wasn't going to be too happy at the sweeping up she'd have to do.

Mr Carterton was in the mews. He didn't have his normal clothes on, either, but he wasn't as ragged as Lady Isabella and me. He inspected both of us carefully. My lady put her chin up at that, but she didn't say anything.

"Are you sure you want to do this?" he asked.

My lady hesitated, but I wasn't surprised when she didn't say no. Instead, she asked if I would be safe.

"There are no absolute guarantees in this world, but I will do my best to keep both of you safe."

There was a thoughtful air about him, as if he'd planned things carefully. He had Mr Archer to assist him, too, who knew some big men with cudgels.

Lady Isabella looked at me, and I nodded. It was too late to change my mind now.

The hackney waiting for us was as shabby as yesterday's, but at least it didn't smell. Langton was already sitting beside the driver, and made no move to get down to assist my lady. Mr Carterton walked straight up to it and got in, ignoring us. I giggled at Lady Isabella's shocked expression.

"He looks better than we do, my lady," I whispered. "A man like that wouldn't be polite to the likes of us."

"You'd better call me Bella," she said, once we were on our way. "Not 'my lady'."

I couldn't do that—I'd just have to avoid calling her anything at all.

The journey was much quicker this time, and we were soon getting out of the hackney again. We took a different route, although the street was as narrow and rough as the ones Langton had led us through. And, only a few yards in, a pair of men similar to the ones we'd seen yesterday were taking too much of an interest in us. Then I saw that Mr Archer was one of them, and behind him a larger man with a bent nose.

Mr Carterton walked right up to him. "Jarndyce. Have you got anything for me?"

"Not much." The big man's voice was quiet, but no-one with even half a brain would make the mistake of thinking he was soft. "I found the Dawkins you mentioned, but she don't know where Fletcher lives, just that it's around here somewhere. I didn't go on to Ruby's, like you said."

I was still nervous, but that reassured me. Mr Carterton had made enquiries, and I didn't think many would dare to get on the wrong side of Jarndyce. As we walked along the narrow alleys a few people looked, then turned away.

Mr Archer knocked on a door with paint peeling off it, and when a thin woman opened it, Jarndyce announced that we'd come to see Ruby.

The woman whined about no rent being due, and I looked at Mr Carterton. How did a gentleman like him know a rent collector?

Jarndyce pushed his way in, and my lady followed him. I'd thought it was a boarding house, that perhaps Fletcher rented a room here, or the Billy she'd mentioned. But the smell didn't fit. It was like being by a privy with the wind in the wrong direction, and something else as well. Sickly and sweet.

"Smells like the paregoric my grandad used for his rheumatics," I said. "Plenty of laudanum in it." Then a baby wailed, and my lady pushed her way into the room the sound came from.

There were rows of babes on the floor, and most needing their clouts changing, by the smell. It almost made me gag, and Lady Isabella looked like she was about to cast up her accounts, but she put a hand to her mouth and managed not to.

Billy must be Fletcher's child, not an adult, if this was where she'd sent Langton with a message. And she was Miss Fletcher, so the babe was a bastard.

Langton had worked it out, too; his sneer made that obvious. Fletcher could have been foolish—or wanton, I suppose, which is what Langton must have assumed. But that wasn't the only possible explanation, and *I* wasn't going to judge until I knew the story.

By now Jarndyce had found out where to look for Fletcher, so we all trooped off again. This time Mr Carterton stopped at the entrance to an alley, sending Mr Archer and Jarndyce to make enquires.

"Mr Carterton—those babies, why were they there?" Lady Isabella asked. "Why did the house smell of paregoric?"

"Ruby looks after them while their parents work. The laudanum in the paregoric stops them crying."

Poor little mites—what chances would they have, with a start in life like that?

"Does that happen in Over Minster?" Lady Isabella asked me.

"Not that I know of, m…" I'd almost called her my lady. "Er, Bella. There's more like to be grandmas to watch the little ones, or older sisters who don't work yet. And they can take babies out to the fields with them if the weather's not too bad."

"The children at Ruby's will be put to work as soon as they're old enough," Mr Carterton said. "As climbing boys for chimney sweeps, or trained as pick-pockets or thieves."

"Oh. Fletcher left him… Billy… there?" I could see my lady didn't think much of Fletcher for leaving a babe in such a place.

"I reckon Fletcher didn't have a choice," I said. "That Madame

Donnard wouldn't have let her have Billy at work, no matter how quiet he was."

She had more questions, I could tell, but Jarndyce came back. He'd found where Fletcher was lodging, and Mr Carterton told us to wait outside while he went in with Mr Archer.

They were gone for five minutes or so, then Mr Archer came down. "You can go up," he said, looking at Lady Isabella. She went in, and Mr Archer jerked his head for me to follow her. We went right up to the top floor, where Mr Carterton and Fletcher were waiting by an open door. She looked even worse than last time I'd seen her, with dark shadows under her eyes and lank wisps of brown hair escaping from her cap.

Lady Isabella followed them into the room. I couldn't see much through the open doorway, but enough to tell that Fletcher's lodging was only one room. There was some talk that I couldn't make out, and then my lady came out again, carrying a bundle of cloth. Fletcher came behind with a babe in her arms. A babe who slept all the way back to the hackney, and slept on in the carriage.

Lady Isabella and I were sent straight upstairs as soon as we got back to Lady Tregarth's house, and a woman who I guessed was the housekeeper took Fletcher and Billy away.

"The boy—do they always sleep so soundly?" my lady asked, once she had washed and put on her clean chemise and I was combing out her hair.

She'd not had anything to do with babies, otherwise she'd never have asked that question. "Things'd be easier if they did, my lady. When I was looking after our little ones, they were always making a fuss. I reckon Billy was given gin or laudanum, same as the others."

She twisted her head around, and I dropped the comb rather than pull her hair.

"I don't reckon Fletcher had a choice there, either," I said. "If the babe was crying too much, other folks in the building would complain." Not like the grand folk, with the nursery far enough away from the main rooms that babies couldn't be heard, no matter how loud they cried.

"Oh. Molly, do you think the baby is a—?"

"You'd have to ask Fletcher, my lady." I didn't want to start talking about base-born children until I knew how Fletcher had come to have Billy. "But even if it was her fault she had the little mite, she's tried hard to look after him. There's some as would just let him die, or leave him at a workhouse." Respectable or not, earning her living with a needle or on her back would be much easier without a babe to look after.

Lady Isabella didn't twist around this time, but her face in the mirror showed her shock. I finished her hair and helped her into her gown before sending her down to Lady Tregarth. I cleaned myself up as best I could, making my fingers sore with scrubbing the dirt from my nails, and went to see how Fletcher was getting on.

A maid directed me to the housekeeper's room, and I knocked. It was Fletcher's voice that said, 'Come in,' and I found her sitting at a round table holding the babe in her arms and trying to feed him with a spoon. A bowl of soup and a plate of buttered bread on the table looked like they hadn't been touched.

"Is he all right?" I drew up another chair, and sat down next to her. "Shall I feed him while you eat? I used to help look after my brother's little ones."

"He's still drowsy." She bumped his lips gently with the spoon, and his mouth opened, but then he waved his arms and the bit of milk-soaked bread fell onto his dress. Not for the first time, either, by the looks of it. I held my arms out. She looked doubtful for a moment, then handed Billy to me. "I've been feeding him as much as I can," she said.

"Best let him wake up properly." He was alert enough to turn his head towards my voice, but then went back to sleep. "You eat, Miss Fletcher. You need it, too."

"Sarah. My name is Sarah." She smiled, although her lips wobbled a little, then started on the soup.

"Molly Simons." Billy began to whimper, so I tried him with

another bit of soggy bread. He ate it this time, and I carried on until the bowl was empty.

The door opened without a knock, and the housekeeper came in. She was younger than Mrs Wardle, and more cheerful-looking, too. "I'll get some more food sent in soon," she promised, when she saw the empty plates. "But best not to eat too much at once. A bath next, I think." She turned to me. "Simons, Lady Isabella is to stay to dinner with Lady Tregarth. She said you may remain here or return to Marstone House."

"I'll stay, for a while. I can look after Billy while Sarah bathes."

"That will be very helpful, thank you." She had a friendly smile—and there were many who wouldn't have been polite to Sarah, what with having Billy, no matter what their mistress said.

A few minutes later a couple of maids came in with a bath, which they set in a corner of the room, then returned with a screen and towels, followed by buckets of steaming water. That kind of thing was normally a footman's job—but if Sarah hadn't had Billy by choice, the last thing she'd want was curious footmen coming in. My estimation of the housekeeper went up even more.

The bundle Lady Isabella had carried was on the floor beside Sarah's chair. She unwrapped it and put a half-sewn shirt on the table, and a little bag that I guessed contained her pins and needles. Then she shook out a clean chemise and hung it over the screen.

"Are you sure you don't mind—?"

"Of course not. Get in the tub while the water's hot—then you can dip Billy in when it's cooler." I wouldn't have minded a bath to rid myself of the stink of the baby house, but that was probably more in my mind than on my skin. Sarah disappeared behind the screen while I dandled Billy on my knee. Sarah eventually appeared with wet hair—pretty hair, it would be when it dried, a soft brown falling halfway down her back. She took Billy, which I wasn't sorry for as my nose was telling me he needed a clean clout.

By the time Billy was changed and clean, the two maids were back with a platter of cold meats and cheeses, more buttered bread, and a large pot of tea. Sarah put a hand to her mouth as the maids set the food out, saying they'd be back later for the bath. Then she was crying; she made no sound, but tears ran down her cheeks.

I took Billy from her and put him down on the rug, then dragged my chair next to hers and put one arm around her shoulders. Ma always said it was best to cry things out, so I just kept an eye on Billy. He looked to be old enough to crawl, but after a bit of looking around and arm waving, he stuck one thumb in his mouth and closed his eyes. At least this might be a natural sleep.

"Lady Isabella came into St Giles to find me." She spoke as if she couldn't believe it, and I didn't blame her.

"Yes. A stupid thing for a lady like her to do."

That earned a faint chuckle. "She's very kind."

"She is, yes." And headstrong. I suspected Sarah was feeling guilty that my lady had gone to so much trouble, so I wasn't going to mention our first trip.

"Who was that gentleman with her?"

"A friend of the family." I guessed she meant Mr Carterton. It was a shame my lady had taken a fancy to that Portuguese—someone like Mr Carterton would make her a much better husband. And Lord Marstone was more likely to allow it, as well.

"Will she be in trouble? I mean, I'm not really a proper person for a young lady to know…" She looked at Billy, and went to pick him up. I moved my chair back and poured the tea—good and strong by now. Sarah settled Billy on her lap again, and bounced him gently while pushing the plates beyond his reach.

"How did you come to have him?" I wished I hadn't asked when her lips turned down at the corners. "It's none of my bus—"

"It is, though. Or Lady Isabella's, after she…" She rubbed her free hand over her eyes. "It was one of the footmen in my last position. I'd walked out with him a couple of times, and he thought that gave him the right to… to…"

"Bloody men." The footman sounded rather like Barlow, although I don't think Barlow had ever gone that far. Not that I knew about, anyway. "Did your employer blame you?"

She shook her head. "No, not my lady. But Sir… her husband

would have done. My lady had the footman up to explain himself, but he refused to marry me and said I'd led him on. I didn't, though." Billy looked up in alarm at the force in her last words.

"Of course you didn't." I just stopped myself from saying that she was better off without him. She hadn't been, until now. And maybe not even now, although I thought Lady Tregarth was as kind as Lady Isabella, and would help.

"His lordship would have believed the man, though. It's always the way."

That wasn't true—Ma had brought up my brother properly—but it was mostly the case. Langton had assumed the worst right away, and you only had to overhear some of the menservants back at Marstone Park to know many men thought the same.

"There's a footman at Marstone House a bit like that." I told her the story of Barlow and the parcels, and her face lightened a bit. I chattered on about my family and Marstone Park while she polished off the plate of food. I didn't get a chance to ask where she came from, as the housekeeper came back in.

"You're to go and see Lady Jesson tomorrow morning," she said to Sarah. I'd never heard of Lady Jesson, but Sarah nodded as if she recognised the name. "Billy will stay here. I'll have a truckle bed brought in, and you can sleep here."

Sarah grimaced, but hid it quickly. It can't be pleasant to know that you're not considered suitable to mix with the servants. She was looking tired, though, and when the housekeeper had gone I took my leave.

CHAPTER 10

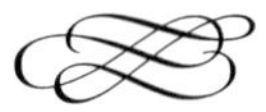

I stood on the pavement outside Lady Tregarth's house, wondering what to do. Lady Isabella wouldn't be needing me for a few hours, and everyone at Marstone House would think I was with her, so I had some time to myself. It was my chance to see a bit more of London. Wandering around the streets would probably get me lost, and I might not come across anything interesting. What I needed was someone who knew their way around.

Sprout was sweeping in Grosvenor Square, as I'd hoped. He came trotting up as soon as he caught sight of me. "Yer got an errand fer me, miss?"

It must be convenient to have such a willing messenger nearby. "How much does Mr Archer pay you to hang around here?"

It was a guess on my part, but he grinned and tapped the side of his nose. "That'd be tellin'."

"Where's a good place to go for a couple of hours? Interesting places to see, I mean." Mr Archer trusted him enough to take messages, so I thought I would be safe with him. I could always turn back if we headed to anywhere like St Giles.

"Park?" he suggested, his face scrunching up in thought.

"That'd be just like the countryside at home."

"The Abbey? Yer seen the river? There's lots more places the nobs go to look at, but yer'd need an 'ackney to get there."

Abbey? Ma had mentioned something like that—a grand version of a church. She'd talked about the size of the river, too, and the stink on hot days. But it wasn't all that warm today. "That'll do. Can you show me the way?"

"Shillin'?"

It would take him a lot longer than running to the Dog and Partridge. "All right." I had plenty left in Mr Archer's purse. This wasn't *quite* what he'd meant the money to be used for, but it wouldn't be missed.

Sprout was an entertaining guide. I learned a lot—not about the fine buildings we passed, or anything about the Abbey, but he told me which street traders would cheat me, which ones were good for a bit of free food at the end of the day, how many children the woman with the basket of oranges had, why I should never wear my pockets outside my skirts…

The Abbey was grand indeed—we could see parts of it sticking above the buildings as we got near, but it wasn't until we got close and I had to lean my head right back to see the tops of the two towers that I realised just how big it was. The church at Over Minster could have fitted into it many times over.

We walked around the outside, gawping at all the fancy carving around the windows and up towards the roof. So many windows! A fine thing it would be to go there on Sundays—there'd be plenty to look at inside while the parson was sermonising. But Sprout's clothes were too dirty and ragged compared to the people going in, and I decided that seeing the inside had best wait for another day.

I'd already missed dinner and tea again, so I gave Sprout more of Mr Archer's money to get us a couple of meat pies. We stood on the nearby bridge to eat them, watching the murky water and the boats going to and fro. He was looking a little rounder of face than when I'd first seen him.

"You making more from Mr Archer than you did sweeping crossings?" I asked.

He nodded. "Me mum didn't 'ave to go out at night this week."

He said it so matter-of-factly that I didn't understand at first. I'd never thought that he might have a family, or even wondered where he slept, and I was ashamed of myself. Billy could have become another Sprout in a few years, without Lady Isabella's interest.

"Time you took me back," I said, licking the last of the gravy from my fingers. When we were back in Grosvenor Square, I gave him an extra shilling. It might give his mum a few more nights off.

Lady Isabella had arranged to go for a drive with Lady Jesson the next afternoon, in Lord Marstone's open carriage, and I was to go with her as far as Lady Jesson's house. We were all ready to go when Lady Cerney called my lady into the parlour, leaving Langton and me in the hall, and the coachman ready outside.

I'd managed to avoid Langton since we arrived back at Lady Tregarth's house the day before, not wanting to hear his opinion of Sarah Fletcher. There was no avoiding it now, though.

"Lady Isabella could have been abducted or killed," Langton said, tilting his head towards the parlour. "She put you in danger, and me. All for the sake of a slut with a bastard child."

Slut?

I took a deep breath, reminding myself that Langton hadn't heard Sarah's story. And that Mowbray was standing near the door and mustn't find out what Lady Isabella had been up to.

"Why does it have to be her fault she had the babe? You don't know anything about her." I hissed the words.

"She's *Miss* Fletcher, isn't she? Didn't manage to trap the father into marrying her, obviously."

I drew in my breath, ready to tell him exactly what I thought of him and his assumptions, but my lady came out of the parlour and I snapped my mouth shut. It was just as well, really—I was that angry I wouldn't have managed to keep my voice quiet.

Even though I hadn't spoken, my expression must have been clear, for he shrugged and went to open the door for Lady Isabella. I followed her out and into the carriage. I was sitting on the back-facing seat, but I kept my eyes on my lady, or on the buildings we passed—anything but Langton standing on his perch behind the carriage. I'd not be able to stop myself looking daggers at him, and then Lady Isabella would ask what was wrong and I couldn't tell her—not with Langton there and the coachman no doubt trying to listen.

It might be a little tricky if my lady needed his help in the future. And to think, I used to wish he'd take a fancy to me.

The carriage pulled up outside Lady Jesson's house and Langton jumped off the back step to knock on the door.

"It does feel grand to be riding in a carriage like this," I said, opening the carriage door ready to get out. Langton wouldn't be handing me down as he would Lady Isabella.

"Stay, Molly," my lady said, as Lady Jesson came out with Sarah Fletcher behind her. "You can come with us, I think."

Sarah was actually looking happy as she settled beside me on the rear-facing seat. Langton, back in his place on the step, had his proper expressionless expression—if that makes sense. But his jaw muscles were tight. I wondered if he was grinding his teeth at the sight of the 'slut' sitting with two proper ladies. I did hope so.

"Do you have a position?" I asked, keeping my voice low so the coachman could not hear. Lady Isabella and Lady Jesson couldn't, either, as they were already talking away together.

Sarah nodded, but her lips wobbled and she pressed them together.

I patted her arm. "Now, there's no reason to cry again!"

"Lady Tregarth and Lady Jesson are so good. And Lady Isabella, of course." She took a deep breath and blinked hard. "Lady Jesson sent Billy to the woman she used as wet nurse for her own boys. And I am to be her personal seamstress for a while."

"Does her own maid not mind?"

"She did, at first, but Lady Jesson said my duties would only be to update her wardrobe." She leaned her head very close to mine. "I think she is not very well off."

And Sarah would make gowns that would suit her for far less than someone like Madame Donnard. Although Lady Jesson looked well enough to me.

"Oh, this is several years out of fashion," Lady Jesson said to Lady Isabella, and I tried not to laugh. The two ladies must have been having a very similar conversation. "I've brought Fletcher along so we can take a look at current fashions. We will dissect everyone's appearance ruthlessly, and both you and I will learn the tricks that will best suit us."

And I would do my best to learn from whatever Sarah said.

Hyde Park didn't look much different from the land around the big house at Marstone Park, with lots of grass and trees. Except for the people—I'd never seen so many fine ladies and gentlemen in one place before. Sarah didn't say much at first, sitting quietly while Lady Jesson and Lady Isabella discussed the redingotes, hair styles, and hats on display.

I wasn't going to learn anything if Sarah didn't speak, and nor would the ladies, so I took things in hand.

"That would look well on you, Lady Isabella." I pointed to a well-endowed lady in a low-cut gown that displayed an awful lot of bosom, with bright embroidery around the neckline drawing attention to the wares on display. A long feather, dyed in the same deep red colour as the gown, curled from her hat towards her neck, and I could imagine men's eyes following that, too.

"Indeed it would," Lady Jesson said. "If she wanted to ruin her reputation."

Lady Isabella gaped for a moment, then giggled. "You didn't mean that, Molly?"

I shook my head as Sarah spoke. "The colour would suit Lady Isabella, although perhaps only as an underskirt, with a lighter over-dress."

"And the hat?" Lady Jesson asked, looking really interested now.

"Too dark for Lady Isabella—she needs a lighter colour to set off her hair. It would look well on you, my lady." Lady Jesson had light brown hair, with only the tiniest dusting of powder.

"Without the feather." Lady Jesson nodded.

"Or a much shorter one." There was no stopping Sarah after that. The ladies pointed out different colours and styles, and Sarah explained why they did or did not bring out the best in the wearers, and how she might adjust them to suit. I'd never remember half of what she said later, but I thought I was beginning to get a better idea of what would suit Lady Isabella, and that was my job. And all the time Langton had to stand on the rear step while two proper ladies talked happily to the woman he'd called a slut. Standing behind them, he didn't have to keep his proper blank footman's face on, and I couldn't help a smirk at his scowl. He saw it, too, which made him frown even more.

There was a pause, and Lady Jesson spoke into the silence. "What is so fascinating that two of you must needs stare at it?" Both Lady Isabella and Sarah were looking at a carriage some distance off—but not so far that I couldn't see that Portuguese standing nearby and watching as it drew away.

"That was Lady Milton, I think," Lady Jesson added.

"Yes, my lady," Sarah said. "She was my last mistress."

I looked with more interest, then, but it was too far for me to make out what the lady was wearing.

"Is she the one who turned you off, Fletcher?" Lady Isabella asked, her voice only just loud enough to hear.

"She had no choice, my lady. No-one will have a maid who's with child. She gave me some money, and a character, but that wasn't any use when I was increasing and then had a babe to look after."

"Who was that with her?" Lady Jesson asked. "I'm sure I've seen him before."

"Senhor da Gama," my lady replied. "The son of a Portuguese viscount." She blushed a little, and Lady Jesson raised an eyebrow. I suspected she didn't miss much.

"Lady Brigham introduced him to society," Lady Isabella went on. "He said Lady Milton was a family friend."

"I didn't hear of any Portuguese connections when I was working there," Sarah said.

He was too smooth when I first saw him, and now it seemed there might be something dubious about him as well as him being too full of himself and hot-headed.

"Hmm," Lady Jesson said. "I always thought Sir Edward didn't pay her enough attention. Spends too much time at Whitehall, from what I've heard."

What was at Whitehall? Lady Isabella's frown said that she didn't know either, so I asked for both of us.

"It's where a lot of government offices are," Lady Jesson explained. "Sir Edward has a position in the Admiralty."

That sounded important—and useful. I couldn't help thinking about Lord Marstone, who spent his time eating and drinking, and making Lady Isabella's life miserable. He was the opposite of useful. I hoped he didn't recover too quickly.

Another open carriage pulled up beside Fancy Man. The lady in it wore a gown as low-cut as the first one we'd discussed. She extended her hand over the side and Fancy Man bowed over it.

"That's Lady Sudbury," Lady Jesson said. "*Not* another family friend, I suspect."

Lady Isabella's lips pressed together as Lady Sudbury raised a hand in farewell to the Portuguese. "She could be. Many men kiss a lady's hand, do they not?"

I'm sure they did, but there was something in the way Lady Sudbury had looked at Fancy Man that made me think it was more than that. And he was encouraging her. I was pleased Lady Isabella had seen something of what he was really like, but not that she was distressed about it. I did wonder, though, whether I might have been a little dreamy too, if he'd turned that melting gaze on me as he had done on my lady. It just went to show that Ma was right when she said you don't want to pick a man because he has a nice face.

Lady Jesson decided she'd seen enough fashions for one day, but I wasn't sure if that was true, or she'd guessed that Lady Isabella was troubled.

I glanced at Langton out of the corner of my eyes as we left the Park—his looks were more to my taste than Fancy Man's.

Not that I was picking a man, of course.

CHAPTER 11

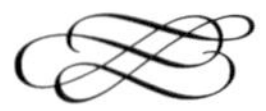

Lady Isabella was to spend the morning with Lady Tregarth the next day. In the carriage on the way there, she asked me to call on Sarah while she was with Lady Tregarth, to see how she was getting on. "I first met Lady Jesson on the day Mr Carterton took us to St Giles," she explained. "Lady Tregarth likes her, but I don't know Lady Tregarth very well, either, so I want to be sure they really are doing the right thing by Fletcher."

"I'll see her, my lady, don't you worry." I wanted to know for myself that Sarah was being treated well.

"Fletcher is more likely to be honest with you, Molly, I think."

My lady probably had the right of it there, and I was happy to do as she asked.

"Does Lady Jesson live far from here?" she asked Lady Tregarth's butler as he took her redingote. We'd called at her house in the carriage the day before, but neither of us knew London well enough to work out how to get there from Lady Tregarth's house.

"Only a few minutes' walk, my lady."

"Thank you. Can you give my maid directions?"

"I will send a footman to show her. This way, if you please, my lady."

She inclined her head, and the butler showed her into a parlour.

Five minutes later I was descending the area steps at Lady Jesson's house and knocking on the door. A scullery maid took me to the housekeeper.

"Lady Isabella asked me to give a message to Miss Fletcher," I said, not sure if a call between friends would be allowed. I didn't want to get Sarah in trouble on only her second day.

The housekeeper nodded. "She's turned a bedchamber into a sewing room. Annie will show you the way." She waved a hand and returned her attention to an account book. She didn't look as cheerful as Lady Tregarth's housekeeper, but she didn't show any signs of disapproval when I mentioned Sarah's name. That was promising.

I found Sarah in a room with the bed pushed into one corner, and a large table in the centre. The pieces of fabric spread out on it looked like a gown partly taken apart.

I explained why I was there—the truth this time—and leaned over to inspect the material. "I'm not interrupting you, am I?"

"I should be working," she said, doubt in her voice. "I must not repay Lady Jesson's kindness by—"

"I'll help."

"Thank you." She handed me a tiny pair of scissors. "I need the rest of this skirt unpicking."

The fabric was rich, shiny, silk brocade, embroidered with swirls of leaves in a contrasting colour. "Lovely material." I bent over the table, careful to slice through the stitches, not the fabric.

"It is. Lady Jesson suggested I start by seeing if I can make up new gowns from old ones. This needs the skirts narrowing, and I will reshape the neckline, too."

The skirts I could deal with, but remaking a bodice was beyond me, and I watched with interest as Sarah marked lines with chalk, using a long strip of paper to check her work. I didn't talk while she was cutting—Ma always said that was the most important part to get right. Measure twice, cut once.

Eventually Sarah stood and straightened her back. "It just needs pinning now. It's so much easier, having my lady available for fittings every day."

"Are they treating you well here? The other servants, I mean."

"Oh yes. Well, they're a bit suspicious—it's not usual to employ a seamstress in the house—but they're all polite."

It sounded rather lonely to me, but it was still far better than her previous situation. "How is Billy? Lady Isabella wanted to be sure you were *both* settled."

"Happy enough." She looked over the fabric on the table. "When do you need to return?"

"A couple of hours. Is he close by?"

"About ten minutes. If you don't mind doing some sewing when we return, we could go to Mrs Leggett's now if you wish?"

The street she led me to was narrow, and lined with small houses—but there were no piles of stinking rubbish like there had been in St Giles. Apart from the usual horse droppings, anyway. Most of the houses looked in good repair, and the front door Sarah knocked on had been painted recently.

A small girl in a yellow frock opened the door, smiling when she saw Sarah. "Me mum's in the kitchen."

The house was sparsely furnished but clean—it would even have met with Ma's approval. The girl disappeared once she'd shown us the way.

Mrs Leggett was a short woman, with a cheery smile and dark hair beneath her cap. "Billy's in the front room." She pointed the way with the knife in her hand.

"This is my friend, Molly Simons. I hope you don't mind her visiting?"

"No, no. You go on." She flapped a hand at us and carried on chopping vegetables.

"Her husband's a sailor," Sarah said, as we went into the parlour. The girl was sitting on the floor, pushing coloured wooden blocks towards a child sitting on a rug. Billy lay asleep in a crib, but opened his eyes as Sarah spoke; he gave a smile that was all gums and dribble, and waved his arms. Sarah picked him up and cooed at him, and a lump formed in my throat at the happiness on her face.

"Mrs Leggett said she lived in when she was the wet nurse for Lady Jesson's boys," Sarah said. "I'd never have sent Billy to that place if I hadn't had to—"

"Of course you wouldn't."

Billy waved his arms again and began to whine. Sarah set him on the floor and he rolled over onto his tummy. He'd be crawling soon, and I wondered how the girl would manage with two little ones. Without the paregoric, I was sure. We spent another ten minutes there, then set off back.

Lady Jesson was alighting from a hackney as we approached the house. Sarah curtseyed. "Molly called, my lady, so I took her to see Billy instead of going this afternoon."

She smiled. "I trust you will give a good report to Lady Isabella?"

I dropped my gaze, embarrassed that she'd so easily guessed my purpose.

Lady Jesson chuckled. "Don't look so embarrassed, my dear. Lady Isabella and I hardly know each other yet, although I'm sure we will be great friends."

She nodded, and climbed the front steps as we went down to the area door.

Lady Isabella went out with Lady Cerney later that afternoon, and Tamworth found me another book to read while my lady was out. Then I had to dress her for an evening at Vauxhall. I'd learned that there were pleasure gardens there, but that didn't mean very much to me. The only gardens I knew were the ones in the village, or the patterns made by low hedges at Marstone Park.

I wondered who else she would be meeting. She was in London to find a husband, but the only men she'd mentioned to me were Mr Carterton and Fancy Man—and I'd lay money that her father wouldn't approve of the Portuguese. She looked a bit distracted when she returned, but was happy enough to describe the place when I asked.

"It was lovely," she said, sitting at her dressing table ready for me to comb out her hair. "There's a big rotunda—a round building—in the middle, with an orchestra playing. There are trees everywhere, with walks between them. And lanterns—Molly, they were like stars everywhere—you should see them!"

I wished I could. "Doesn't sound like a place for the likes of me, my lady."

"Oh, anyone can go. Lord Barnton told me a lot about the different buildings and paintings." Her bottom lip came out.

"Lord Barnton? Is he one of your suitors?"

Her sigh wasn't a dreamy one—not like when she mentioned Senhor da Gama. "I think so, but he's… not very interesting."

I'd gathered that she didn't think Mr Carterton was very interesting, either, so that didn't tell me much about Lord Barnton. But she was yawning, and I didn't think I'd get much more from her that evening.

Things changed the next day; I told my lady the news as I was dressing her. "Mrs Wardle's told the maids to get Lord Marstone's room ready, my lady. He's expected this afternoon."

She twisted round as I was trying to brush her hair. "My aunt didn't say anything about him coming."

"A letter came yesterday, from what I heard. Now hold still, my lady, do."

She sat in silence while I dressed her hair up, gazing into the mirror, and a little crease formed between her brows.

"Molly, can Langton get a message to Mr Carterton?"

"Already done, my lady." He'd done it before I asked him. "And Langton'll do his best to listen to any talk." I hadn't asked him that, but I knew he would.

She glanced towards the closet where I'd hidden her maid's clothing. "Do you know the servants' passages here?"

I could find the way to places where she might be able to eavesdrop on Lord Marstone, but I didn't trust the likes of Barlow not to spy on us. "Not well, my lady, nor yet the routines, not properly. You're like to get caught if you try listening at doors. I'll see what I can find out for you, but Mrs Wardle keeps a close eye on things."

I took her night clothes into the dressing room to air them, and my lady had gone down for her breakfast when I returned to the bedroom. But she wasn't away long.

"My redingote and bonnet, Molly, quickly."

"My lady?" I hurried over to the closet.

"I need to see Lady Jesson. I sent her a note to say I'd call after my dancing lesson, but Aunt Aurelia wants me to go on calls with her then, so I must go now. You'd better come, too."

I held the redingote for her, but she waved me off. "I can do that—go and get your outdoor things."

I didn't know Lady Isabella could walk so fast. My legs were longer than hers, but I struggled to keep up. At Lady Jesson's house, I sat on a chair in the hallway while my lady vanished into a parlour. I thought it best not to go and talk to Sarah—I'd be taking too much of her time, but also my lady was like to be in a hurry to get back as soon as she'd finished with Lady Jesson.

A clock on a little table ticked away, chiming the quarter hour, then the half-hour, before Lady Jesson emerged with Lady Isabella behind her. But they kept going, into another room across the hall, and it must have been another ten minutes before my lady was ready to leave.

"Is everything all right, my lady?" I ventured, as we set off again, not quite so fast this time.

"No."

Well, I suppose it *had* been a silly question.

"My aunt said that father wants a list of my suitors. He's in a hurry to see me wed."

"Lord Barnton," I suggested.

"And Lord Narwood, if he has written to Papa." She hadn't mentioned that lord before, but her face said it all.

"You don't like him."

"He's old—older than my father. And I… well, I don't like the way he looks at me."

I knew the feeling—few maids didn't. But avoiding lecherous footmen was one thing; being married to such a man and completely in his power was likely worse. I wanted to know what she'd talked about with Lady Jesson, but it wasn't my place to ask. Besides, if her plan involved me, I'd find out soon enough.

Lord Marstone arrived in the middle of the afternoon, while Lady Isabella was out with Lady Cerney. I stayed well out of the way while all the fuss of settling his lordship into his room went on. Whatever had ailed him a couple of weeks ago must still have been giving him trouble, for Cook was told that his lordship would be having his meals in his room.

I'd just left my lady's room later, on my way to the servants' hall, when I heard Lady Cerney's voice. "…no reason why we could not have this interview after we finished dinner."

Lord Marstone must have summoned her. His room was on the floor below Lady Isabella's, and I ran along to the main staircase and looked over the banister. Lady Cerney was turning into that corridor, with Lady Isabella trailing behind her. My lady was looking apprehensive, but not as much as I thought she would. I wondered what plan she and Lady Jesson had come up with.

I hurried down and peered along the corridor. Chambers—Lord Marstone's valet—stood outside his lordship's room, blocking Lady Cerney's way. He was speaking, but not loudly enough for me to make out his words clearly. Something about not angering Lord Marstone. As if it took much to get his lordship into a temper!

Lady Cerney gave him one of her looks. Chambers bowed and stepped back, and they all went in.

The servants' stair opened onto the corridor not far from his lordship's room. I'd probably find out what his lordship had to say from Lady Isabella later, but I was curious. I wanted to know now. Taking a chance, I crept along the corridor and pushed the door. It stopped when it was only open a few inches, and someone swore.

"Let me in," I whispered urgently. I had no business in this corridor and didn't want to get caught if Chambers came out of his lordship's room. The door opened and I slipped through; Langton pushed it to again, leaving only a narrow gap.

"I'll listen," he hissed. "You don't need to."

I shook my head and leaned so my ear was close to the gap between the door and the frame, trying to hear something—anything—from his lordship's room.

Langton said nothing else, but leaned in as well. I tried to ignore him, but having him so close was making me feel uncomfortable, his warm breath tickling my ear. A strange feeling, it was, not at all like when Barlow made me squeeze past him by blocking my way.

It was all for nothing, though—we couldn't hear anything through his lordship's door, and after only about five minutes the ladies came out and went downstairs. Langton straightened up.

"Molly, what did—?"

"Have you overheard anything useful?"

"No, but—"

"If it's not to do with Lady Isabella, I don't want to hear it." I set off up the stairs, not waiting for him to reply. After a moment I heard his own footsteps descending. But as I went on up, I wished I'd not been quite so hasty. Had he been about to ask what had happened to Sarah?

Lady Isabella's gown for that evening's ball was a delicate pink over an ivory petticoat embroidered in the same pink. Ivory lace around the neck and short sleeves finished it off, and she wore a single stranded pearl necklace. She sat in silence, staring into the mirror as I wove another strand of pearls in her hair, with a few tiny silk flowers.

She looked lovely, but only nodded at her reflection when I said so. Lord Marstone could put a damper on anything—my lady should be looking forward to her first ball, but her father had spoiled it.

"What did his lordship say?" I ventured finally.

"He was angry that there is no suitable marriage arranged yet." Her lips curved, but it wasn't a proper smile. "Aunt Aurelia gave him a long list of my suitors—I hope he doesn't find out that she invented most of them."

"Lady Cerney did that?" I hadn't thought she'd go in for that kind of deception.

"It was Lady Jesson's idea." Her eyes met mine in the mirror, and there was a brief hint of laughter in hers.

"Has that Lord Narwood written to him, as you feared, my lady?"

"No—but he might still do so." She took a deep breath and stood, hands smoothing her skirts. "Lady Jesson had some other ideas, if this one fails."

Running away was the only one that came to my mind, but my lady had tried that with her sisters two years ago and had got no further than the nearest coaching inn. That was back when I was still helping Betsy to look after all three young ladies.

Lady Isabella had more folks who would help her now, though. Mr Carterton and Mr Archer should be able to get her to Lord Wingrave's place, but would Lord Marstone send someone after them?

CHAPTER 12

I knew something was wrong as soon as Lady Isabella returned that evening. She fidgeted with the jars on her dressing table as I was unpinning her hair, and when I'd finally got her into her night things, instead of getting into bed she went into the dressing room and started to look through her gowns.

"My lady?" She surely didn't want to get dressed again?

"Lord Narwood said he will write to Papa," she said. "I… I have a plan, but I don't know if it will work. I might need to go to Devonshire. If I can reach Ashton Tracey, Lady Wingrave can help me until Will returns."

"What about Mr Carterton, my lady?" He would help her.

"I do not intend to run away on my own, Molly. I've learned that lesson."

"Well, even if Lord Narwood writes this evening, his lordship won't get the letter until the morning, at the earliest. You'll make better plans if you've had some sleep." I took the gown she was holding and put it away.

She rubbed her eyes. "You're right, of course. But bring my chocolate early, Molly. I'm probably going to need your help again."

"You only need to ask, my lady. Shall I bring you some hot milk?"

"Thank you, but no."

I left her climbing into bed and went up to my own, wondering what mad plan she'd try this time. Whatever it was, I hoped it would work better than the last.

As she'd requested, I took her morning chocolate a little earlier than usual. She was already awake, writing a letter.

"This is for Archer, Molly, and I will write to Lady Jesson too. Can you get Langton to deliver them?"

"What's the plan, my lady?"

"There isn't one, not yet. But I want to warn them that I might need their assistance. Then you can help me to pack a trunk, and put in some of your own things, too." She turned on her chair to face me. "You *will* come with me, won't you? My brother will—"

"I know, my lady. Of course I'll come—can't let you go traipsing around the country on your own, can I?" I didn't want to, but I couldn't let her go without me, either.

"Thank you." She looked a little happier at my answer, but not much. "Langton will have to get the trunk out of the house before my father suspects I might try to run away again."

"I'll tell him, my lady." I'd best give the letters to Sprout, if he was around. Langton would have enough to do getting the trunk away, without having to deliver messages as well.

When the letters were ready I put on my pelisse and bonnet and headed out to the square. I was prepared to say that Lady Isabella had sent me to match ribbon, but no-one asked what I was about. Sprout was lurking on the corner—I crooked a finger and walked off in the opposite direction, and he joined me once I was out of sight of Marstone House.

"One for Mr Archer." I handed it over. "And one for Lady Jesson, on Henrietta Street. Do you know where that is?"

"Yeah."

"Can you read?" I suddenly wondered if he'd get the right letters to the right people—my lady wouldn't want Mr Archer reading what she might have said to Lady Jesson.

"Course I can't," he said scornfully. He held up one of the letters. "But I can remember this one's for Mr Archer."

It was. Reassured, I handed over some coins, and he set off at a brisk trot.

Lady Cerney was to take Lady Isabella on calls again that afternoon. His lordship hadn't sent any messages, so I helped her change into a new walking dress. We were downstairs in the hall waiting for Lady Cerney when Mowbray came down the stairs.

"Lord Marstone wishes to see you in his study, Lady Isabella."

"I am on my way out, Mowbray. Can it not wait?" But she pulled on her bonnet ribbons and handed it to me before he answered. There wasn't any point in protesting against his lordship's orders. Mowbray escorted her up the stairs.

I didn't bother trying to listen at the door this time, not with Mowbray likely lingering in the passage in case he was wanted, so I went back to my lady's bedchamber to tidy up. The first I knew that things had gone wrong was when Lady Isabella came back in with Mowbray behind her. She stopped in the doorway and turned to face him.

"I trust you will post someone in the corridor, to let Molly in or out."

What?

"My lady, his lordship did not—"

"My father did not say I was to be starved, did he? Or denied the services of my maid?"

"No, my lady." I'd never seen Mowbray shuffle his feet before.

"Then see that Molly *can* come and go, as I require."

She didn't wait for him to answer, but stepped into the room and shut the door in his face—looking very like Lady Cerney when she was displeased.

There was silence for a moment, then the key scraped in the lock. Suddenly my lady looked like a young girl again, and sank into a chair.

I didn't say anything for a minute, just carried on tidying. Well, moving things around, really, but I didn't want my lady to think she had to tell me. But she did, of course.

"Lord Narwood *has* written to my father. Papa was talking about getting a special licence—I could have been married to him within a couple of days."

I didn't know what to say. Then I realised she'd said 'could have been', not 'will be'.

"What did you do, my lady?"

"I… I suggested that I might be with child."

No—she could not be! She would not do such a thing, any more than I would.

"I'm not, of course…"

Thank heavens.

"…but I persuaded my aunt to help me to convince him that I am. And that if he does insist on the match, Lord Narwood—and everyone else—will soon find out that my first child will not be his."

"But my lady, if everyone—"

"I know, Molly. But unless my father is very foolish, he will refuse Narwood and no-one will know what I said."

"What will he do now? How long are you to be locked in for?"

"I don't know. He might send me back to Marstone Park while he tries to arrange another match."

Who would want a bride carrying a child by another man? Then I remembered how rich Lord Marstone was. There'd be a lot of men hungry for the money and the link with an earl. And none of them the kind of man Lady Isabella would be happy married to.

"I can't do anything now," she went on, "but tonight… Tonight we might see if you can get the key, or bribe whoever is left in the corridor."

. . .

Later that afternoon I was allowed down to the kitchens to fetch tea and some food. No-one seemed inclined to talk to me directly—not even Langton, who might at least have asked after my lady. I remembered how I had cut him off on the stairs the day before and had the uncomfortable feeling that the estrangement between us was partly my fault now.

While I was waiting for the kitchen maid to bring cold meat and cheese from the larder, I overheard talk about a doctor being summoned. I had a sudden fear that he was to examine Lady Isabella to see if her story was true, but it seemed that his lordship had worked himself into a temper again. Not long after we'd finished eating, Barlow came to tell Lady Isabella that Lord Marstone and Lady Cerney wished to see her, and he was to escort her to her father's room. Apart from a sneer, he ignored me—which suited me well.

I waited until they were on the stairs, out of sight, and then let myself into the servants' stair, creeping down to the floor below as quietly as I could. I *was* going to try to listen again this time, in case I wasn't allowed back with Lady Isabella.

Peering through the gap between the almost-closed door and the frame, I watched as Lady Isabella entered the room and Barlow closed the door and leaned on the wall beside it.

Nothing happened for some time, then Lady Cerney opened the door, my lady close behind her.

"Aurelia, come back here! I've *told* you not to walk away while I'm talking to you." It was his lordship's voice, loud enough to hear, but only just. He must be ill indeed—his ranting could usually be heard several rooms away. Lady Cerney closed the door and walked off down the corridor with Lady Isabella and Barlow behind them.

I managed to get back into my lady's bedchamber before they reached the upper corridor, and hid in the dressing room without closing the door completely. I didn't want anyone to suspect I'd been trying to listen—for all the good it had done me!

Lady Cerney followed Lady Isabella into the room, and Barlow cleared his throat. "Er, excuse me, my lady."

"Yes? What is it?"

"His lordship said no-one was to talk to Lady Isabella."

There was silence, and I imagined Lady Cerney giving him her stare. Then he apologised, and the door slammed—with Barlow on the other side of it, I guessed.

"I wouldn't put it past that insolent lackey to listen." That was Lady Cerney's voice, faint, as if she was on the far side of the room. Very sensible—Barlow *would* be trying to listen. Well, so was I, but I was going to be helping my lady, not tattling to her father.

"Isabella, I cannot let you run off unprotected." Lady Cerney's voice became even quieter, and I strained to hear it. Did that mean she was going to stop my lady, or help her? "You are thinking of that, aren't you?" she went on. "I cannot take you home with me—Cerney would not like to get involved in a dispute with Marstone."

"Papa would have me brought back, anyway." Lady Isabella sounded despondent, which wasn't surprising, considering. I supposed Lord Marstone could have her brought back from her brother's place in Devonshire, too, but Lord Wingrave would make more of an effort to prevent it.

"Yes. He has the right, in law..." Lady Cerney's voice became indistinct. If I moved any closer to the door I risked pushing it closed, and although Lady Cerney seemed to be sympathetic, I didn't want to be getting one of her glares for listening. They talked on, voices only a murmur, until finally I heard them moving.

"Yes, the sooner the better, I think," Lady Cerney said. "Do take care, my dear."

The door to the corridor opened and closed, and the key turned in the lock. I stepped into the room, wary of my lady's reaction, but she only beckoned me over to the window and sat on the window seat. "How much did you hear, Molly?"

"Not all that much, my lady."

She patted the cushion beside her. "Come and sit here. We must be quiet."

"Will she help you?"

"A little, yes. She is to arrange for Langton to be on duty outside the door tonight, so we can all go to Lady Jesson when the rest of the house is asleep."

"Not to Mr Carterton?"

She shook her head.

"Why not Mr Carterton? Will he not help?"

"He would if I asked him—I think. But I don't want to… to…" She sighed. "I'd better tell you the whole story."

"That's all right. We're not going anywhere." It wasn't funny, really, but she managed a little smile.

"My father wanted me to marry the father of my child—that is, the one I told him I was expecting. I told him it was Senhor da Gama."

I nodded, but didn't say anything. Getting a young lady with child seemed the kind of thing Fancy Man might do.

"I also informed Papa that Senhor da Gama is the illegitimate son of a Spanish nobleman."

Fancy Man was a bastard?

"What's he doing in England, then?" Apart from trying to seduce ladies. "And I thought he was Portuguese, not Spanish?"

"Spying. He was only pretending to be Portuguese."

My mouth must have fallen open—Lady Isabella was watching me with a slight curve to her lips.

"He wasn't a very good spy," she added. "And I think he's going back to Spain."

"But your father wouldn't want you to marry a bast— Someone like that, I mean."

"No. He is sending me back to Marstone Park until he can find someone to marry me. Anyone will do, probably, as long as they are respectable." Her voice became more urgent, but she managed to keep it quiet. "Molly, once I'm back at Marstone Park I'll have no escape. I have to leave now, while Lady Jesson and Archer can help me. I… I don't want to ask Mr Carterton, because if Papa finds out, he'll make it seem like Mr Carterton has ruined my reputation and find some way to force us to marry."

"He seems like a good man, my lady. Not like that Lord Narwood."

"He is a good man—very good. But I want to choose for myself, like my sisters did. It wouldn't be fair to Mr Carterton, either—I think he may be courting someone else."

And who would want Lord Marstone as a father-in-law?

"Are we still to go to Devonshire, my lady? How long will it take?"

"Two or three days, I think. Perhaps a bit less if we travel overnight, but people might remember us more if we do that. Ostlers at the inns, I mean."

People might notice us anyway—I didn't think young ladies like her travelled without a gentleman to escort them. Mr Archer and Langton wouldn't count. Still, there was plenty of time to think about that—we wouldn't be leaving until midnight, or later.

"Let us have some tea, Molly, if you please. And when you fetch it, you might be able to find out if Langton *is* to be on duty tonight."

I knocked on the door to the corridor, saying I wanted to be let out, and the door opened. I'd expected Barlow, so it was a pleasant surprise to see O'Connor instead.

"I'm to fetch tea for my lady."

"All right." He stood back, and locked the door after me. But once I was on the servants' stairs I hesitated, then went up instead of down. The pallet on my bed was too large for me to manage without making a good deal of fuss and bother, but I stripped the sheets and blankets, and picked up the pillow. Balancing my hairbrush and comb on top, I headed back to my lady's room

"What's all that?" O'Connor looked suspicious, as well he might.

"I'm going to tie them together to make a rope so we can escape through the window."

His mouth fell open. "You can't… Oh, you're laughing at me, so you are."

"Only a little." I gave him a friendly smile—we couldn't count on his help, but I didn't think he'd go out of his way to hinder us, either. "You don't want to be opening the door every time my lady wants me, do you? Easier if I sleep in the dressing room until we're back at Marstone Park."

He shrugged, and opened the door. Lady Isabella must have heard, for she didn't question me, and I dropped my things on the dressing room floor.

I stopped by O'Connor again on the way out. "I thought Barlow was standing guard?"

"Lady Cerney complained to Mowbray about him. Don't know what he did, but she said he wasn't to go near her or Lady Isabella. Mowbray set him to clean all the silver, whether it needs it or not." He shuffled from one foot to the other. "To be honest, I'd rather be doing that. No-one to talk to here, and nothing to see."

"Oh, well. You won't be here all night."

"Some of it," he said, with a grimace. "Langton's to do eight until two, then I've to get up and take over. Wish *I'd* annoyed Lady Cerney!"

I patted his arm. "Never mind. We'll probably be off to Marstone Park tomorrow."

I still had my lady's tea to fetch. Langton came through the kitchen while the maid was setting the things out on the tray, and I met his eyes and gave a tiny jerk of my head. He came over straight away, which was a relief—I'd hoped our falling out wouldn't prevent him helping Lady Isabella. The maid soon came back with the tray, but I just had time to tell him that my lady wanted to leave tonight. He nodded, with a grimace that he quickly wiped off his face before anyone else saw it.

I took the tray upstairs, and Lady Isabella drank her tea. Half an hour later the key turned and someone knocked on the door. It was Langton.

"Got the trunk?"

I pointed to the dressing room door, and followed him across the room. "Where's O'Connor?"

"I said I'd stand guard for half an hour while he has his tea." He took the trunk and locked us in, still with that scowl on his face. It was going to be a long journey to Devonshire if he looked like he'd lost a shilling and found sixpence all the way.

CHAPTER 13

It was one o'clock when Langton scratched quietly on the door and slipped inside without waiting for a response. He must have contrived to oil the lock, for I didn't hear the usual scraping noise.

We were already in our outdoor things—we had been for a couple of hours. My lady hadn't settled to anything while we waited, and she'd had to force herself to eat some of the food sent up at her normal dinner time. I was glad to have some sewing to do, even though it would be left behind—it kept my hands busy.

I tried not to think of what would happen if we were caught. It was all very well Lord Wingrave promising to employ us, but Lord Marstone could do worse than turn us off. If a servant was accused of theft, the constable would believe his lordship or his secretary over a maid, whether or not they were telling the truth. I should have thought of that before, of course, but taking letters to my lady without her father's knowledge was a lot different from helping her to run away. But I'd promised, and I couldn't abandon her now.

Langton put his finger to his lips, but we didn't need telling. We crept down the servants' stairs without a word said, and along the dark passage below stairs. A couple of lamps were always left lit in case of emergencies in the night, turned down low, and they gave just enough light to see.

Mowbray's snores sounded through his closed door, and for a moment they masked the sound of our footsteps. Langton stopped, and my lady and I almost walked into him—but in the sudden quiet, I heard other footsteps.

What was on this corridor? I didn't know, but Langton had worked in this house before, many times, and quickly opened a door opposite Mowbray's and ushered us in.

I tried not to breathe as the footsteps drew closer. Lady Isabella gripped my hand tight. Langton was only a slightly blacker shape in the darkness, blocking most of the dim light that came through the crack in the door. Then a strip of light appeared above him—whoever was coming must be carrying a lantern. At last, the footsteps went past, and I breathed easily again.

"Chambers," Langton whispered. "He's gone into the kitchen."

He must be getting a drink for his lordship. Langton listened for a moment—we all did. All I could hear was my heartbeat in my ears.

"Come." Langton slipped back into the corridor and we followed, doing our best to tread quietly on the stone-flagged floor. Then, finally, we were out into the garden behind the house.

There was a bit of a moon that let us see paths and flower beds. The paths were gravelled, but we trod slowly and didn't make too much noise—not enough to carry through the walls between us and the kitchen. The door in the back wall squeaked, but we were out with it shut behind us before anyone could have got to a window to see what was happening.

Footsteps—running footsteps—sounded on the cobbles, and my heart sped up. My lady gasped.

Then I realised that the sound was getting further away.

"Don't worry, my lady," Langton whispered. "It's only a lad gone to fetch the hackney. Archer arranged for one to be waiting around the corner from midnight. Come, we don't want him noticed by anyone from the house."

He didn't wait for any acknowledgement, but set off along the mews. We arrived at the street as the hackney pulled up.

"Been here for hours," the driver grumbled. No more than an hour, if what Langton had said was true, but waiting always felt longer than it really was.

"You were at home all night," Langton said, low-voiced, as he dropped coins into the man's hand. A lot of coins, for what would be only a short journey.

The driver squinted at the money, then nodded and stowed it in a pocket. Lady Isabella had already climbed inside, so I followed and Langton shut the door on us.

The hackney drew up at Lady Jesson's house, and the front door opened before we'd even got out. It was the butler himself—he peered at Lady Isabella, then threw the door wide.

"Lady Jesson is expecting you, my lady. If you would step this way?" He turned his gaze on me and Langton. "You two as well." If he disapproved of us turning up after midnight, he hid it well.

He led the way along the hall to where Lady Jesson was waiting in an open doorway. "Come in, my dear."

Lady Isabella hesitated. "I don't want to cause trouble with Lord Jesson, my—"

"It wouldn't be trouble, but it is easier to avoid long explanations, so the fewer people who know about this, the better. Do sit down, all of you."

I did as she said, perching on the edge of the chair. It didn't seem right to be sitting in a lady's parlour. Langton had on the blank expression that he wore when he was in the presence of the family, and didn't look any more at ease than I felt.

"Archer has ordered a hired chaise for eight o'clock, he informed me," Lady Jesson said to Lady Isabella. "He will accompany you, along with your maid and footman. He thought it would appear too suspicious, and be more memorable, if you were to set out before dawn."

"If you please, my lady…" I'd been thinking about being noticed.

"Yes, Molly?"

I was impressed that Lady Jesson remembered my name. "If Lord Marstone sends someone to look for Lady Isabella, we... I mean, don't young ladies like Lady Isabella usually have a gentleman or an older lady to accompany them on long journeys?"

"Why yes, but I cannot go with you. It would raise too many questions if I suddenly changed my plans."

"I didn't mean that, my lady. If Lady Isabella doesn't mind..." I was beginning to wish I'd consulted my lady before now, but the idea hadn't come to me until it was nearly time for us to set out. "Lord Marstone's men won't be looking for a couple with a baby. Mr Archer could pretend to be the father."

"Billy Fletcher?" Lady Jesson smiled. "But do you have any experience of looking after a child?"

"Only my brother's children, my lady. But I meant for Sarah to come, to be Mrs Archer. Mr Archer wouldn't sound like Lady Isabella's husband, if someone hears them both speak."

"Am I to be the nursemaid?" Lady Isabella asked. She didn't seem to be offended, as most ladies would be.

"Yes, my lady. You wouldn't have to say anything much."

"That is an excellent idea, Molly," Lady Jesson said. "Well done."

"But Molly must come as well, Maria," my lady said. "I cannot send her back to Marstone House—my father will know she helped me as soon as I am missed."

I could stay at Lady Jesson's house for a while, I supposed. But if I was going to be found a new position by Lord Wingrave, it would be better if I was at his place in Devonshire.

Lady Jesson tapped her chin with a finger. "I don't suppose Archer would pass for gentry, but he might plausibly be a merchant. Wealthy enough to have a nursery maid with him inside the chaise, and a footman and maidservant outside." She turned her attention to Langton, still wearing his livery and wig. "I doubt a merchant would have a footman dressed as finely as you...?"

"Langton, my lady. I have some normal clothing in one of the bags that Mr Archer had delivered."

"Excellent. Molly, please ask my butler to show you where Fletcher's room is, and explain the situation to her. We will need suitable clothing for Lady Isabella—Fletcher can help with that, too."

Half an hour later, my lady was dressed in a plain dark blue gown and white cap. Sarah and I had hurriedly tacked up the hem, as the parlourmaid who'd lent it was rather taller than Lady Isabella. The maid was happy with the promise of a replacement new gown, and a few coins ensured that she wouldn't gossip about the goings on.

Voices in the hall interrupted Lady Jesson as she was trying to persuade my lady to rest in her bedroom. I thought at first that Lord Marstone's men had found us already, but Lady Jesson didn't seem worried. But then, she wouldn't be losing her position or possibly brought up in front of a magistrate.

The door opened and a gentleman walked in. He was friendly-looking, his dark hair tied back without powder and lines beside his eyes that made him look like he smiled a lot. But his neckcloth was loose, his hair was coming out of its queue, and his cheeks looked rather red—drunk, I guessed.

He stopped and gaped when he saw us all gathered in the parlour. "Good grief, Maria, what are you doing?"

"Nothing you need worry about, Jesson. Merely helping a friend."

Lord Jesson gazed from me to my lady, and his brows drew together. I thought he was angry, until he asked which one was the friend.

"Never mind, Jesson." Lady Jesson walked over and took his arm, turning him so he faced the door and giving him a little push. "I'll tell you all about it in the morning, when you're in a fit state to listen."

He laughed, and kissed her on the cheek. "If I remember, my dear!"

Lady Jesson closed the door behind him, and turned to my lady. "Don't worry, Bella. He won't let our secret out intentionally, but I'll make up something that won't put Marstone on your track if he does talk when in his cups."

Did any fine ladies have good husbands? But I'd take someone like Lord Jesson who was happy when drunk over a sober man with a temper, any time.

. . .

The clouds might have let some moonlight through when we left Marstone House, but by morning they had thickened to a grey sheet, threatening rain. The carriage arrived on time, but we were a little delayed in setting out—Billy suddenly needed his clout changing, and I began to wonder whether taking a baby along was a good idea after all.

Mr Archer had hired a chaise, so there was only a single bench inside, where he and my lady sat with Sarah squashed between them. That left the footman's seat at the back for me and Langton.

Some spits of drizzle touched my face as the postboys started the horses. I wished Mr Archer had arranged a bigger carriage, but he hadn't known Sarah was to come with us. I wasn't too worried about being cold, as the air was mild even at this hour. But it might come on to rain before we reached Devonshire, and I didn't fancy being in damp clothes for a couple of days.

I was excited to be going to Devonshire—I'd seen pictures of the sea, of course, but it was difficult to imagine all that water. It was a pity about the weather, though. It would have been grand to see all the new places in sunshine.

We left the fine houses behind us quite quickly, and then there was little to look at but fields and hedges, followed by some wilder country. We passed carts laden with hay or boxes and crates—we were going faster than a lot of them, with four horses and no heavy luggage, but we still had to stop at the toll houses like everyone else.

The journey to London had been much more interesting, with the coachman telling me about the places we saw on the way. I looked at Langton out of the corner of my eyes, wondering if he knew this road and the places on it—and if he would bother to tell me about them if he did. But he was sitting with folded arms and his lips turned down, staring at the road ahead, and I decided it wasn't worth asking.

We pulled into an inn on the edge of a small town—a busy place, with another coach having its horses changed, and a group of people standing around by piles of bags and boxes. Waiting for one of the public coaches, I guessed.

Another coach pulled in behind us—a big one, with shiny paint and a crest on the door. The coachman and two footmen up behind wore splendid livery in red and blue. The ostlers unharnessing our horses left them half undone and hurried across to sort out the new arrival. Two finely dressed ladies got out and went into the inn, holding up their skirts against the muck in the yard. No-one got out of our carriage, which was probably wise. We must still be quite close to London.

We didn't get our horses changed until the fancy coach had left, and a hollow feeling grew in my stomach. I couldn't help wondering if Lady Isabella's escape had been noticed yet. If we were lucky, when O'Connor came to guard the door—*had* come, by now—he would have thought that Langton had gone off to use the necessary or something. And if he was guarding my lady's door, he couldn't be in the servants' hall to notice that Langton wasn't there.

The spatters of drizzle turned to rain as we left that town, and Langton turned his collar up. "All this because Lady Isabella doesn't want to marry the lord her father picked out for her." He'd muttered the words, but I heard them all the same.

"You didn't have to come." Lady Jesson would have lent my lady one of her footmen, or Mr Archer could have hired someone.

"What—I should have stayed behind so Lord Marstone would punish me for letting Lady Isabella out?"

"Didn't say you had to stay in Marstone House, did I?"

"What would Lord Wingrave think if I didn't do my best to help her ladyship?"

I shrugged. "Why does it matter what he'd think? I'd do my best to help her even if Lord Wingrave hadn't promised to look after us. It's not right that she should be forced to wed someone like the one Lord Marstone was wanting."

"She'll have someone to pay her bills, won't she? Isn't that what all women want?"

Need, more than want. It wasn't quite the same thing. "And men just want someone in their beds." Not all men, I knew that. But what else would this Lord Narwood want with my lady, with him being so much older than her? "How would *you* like to be forced to wed someone as old as your grandmother? Or even older? And only to warm her bed?"

"It's not the same at all."

Perhaps it wasn't for men, although I'm not sure I believed him. But there was no point talking if he was going to be like that. I turned my shoulder to him and kept my eyes on the scenery. The rain soon eased off, but there were only more fields and hedges to look at. I whiled away some of the time eating the bread and cheese Lady Jesson's cook had provided, and Langton did the same, but eventually the silence began to bother me. It was hard work ignoring Langton, especially as the bumps kept throwing us together.

And it didn't help that I was wondering whether the pair of us were going to end up in gaol if Lord Wingrave didn't keep his word.

CHAPTER 14

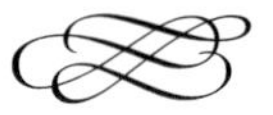

The next time we stopped, I scrambled down from the seat—I needed to use the privy. Mr Archer opened the door and my lady climbed out awkwardly with Billy in her arms. He looked at the ostlers taking the horses away with a frown. I didn't know how far we'd come, but I guessed from his expression that the muddy roads and the stuck cart we'd encountered half an hour ago had slowed us down a lot. Those ostlers didn't look to be moving as fast as they could, either.

Mr Archer turned back to me, his face softening. "All right, Molly?"

I nodded, and he directed me around the back of the inn; by the time I returned, Lady Isabella had got back inside and there were new horses in harness. Langton put his hand down to help me up, but I ignored him, hitching up my skirt to reach the steps.

The coach set off, and Langton folded his arms again. "Are you going to sulk all the way to Devonshire?"

"I'd rather not talk to someone who thinks the worst of people without knowing anything about them."

"What, you're still holding that against me?"

I turned to look at him. "You called my friend a slut."

His brows rose. "Your friend? You didn't even know where she lived."

"She's my friend now."

He didn't reply, and after a moment I looked away.

"You thought the best of her without knowing anything," he said after a while. He sounded like he was just having a chat, not an argument. "Besides, what more do you need to know beyond a bastard child?"

"A man had nothing to do with it then? Funny, that—I thought it took two people to make a baby."

His mouth turned down at the corners. "Women lead men on, and then get with child so they can have a ring on their finger."

"Really?" No doubt some did, but Sarah hadn't. "So you assume that's what Sarah was doing?"

"Well, what was I to think when—?"

"Think? You could have *thought* that you might wait to find out how she came to have Billy before judging. You didn't even bother to ask, did you?"

"Some women do that," he muttered.

"So Sarah must have done? Was I trying to get Barlow to marry me, then, when he tried to put his hand up my skirt?" I remembered what Barlow had told him. "Of course, that *is* what you think, isn't it? And I was so jealous he escaped that I *made* him answer back to Lady Cerney."

There must be some reason for the way Langton thought. Had some woman tried to trap him into marriage? I opened my mouth to ask, then thought better of it. What did it matter where his nasty ideas came from? I'd be sitting beside him for another couple of days, and silence was better than arguing all the way.

"Anyway, whatever you think of Sarah, you'll have to be polite to her when we stop. People are supposed to think you work for her." I hoped the idea annoyed him.

We stopped for longer at the next town, and had dinner in the taproom. My lady made a good job of feeding Billy bits of bread soaked in milk—I don't think she'd even held a baby before this. She didn't eat much herself, though. Not that I blamed her. The beef stew was mainly grease and soggy bits of turnip, and the bread felt like it had been sliced that morning and left out to dry. The place was noisy, so there was no chance to talk, even if any of us had wanted to.

The silence between me and Langton lasted all the way to Reading, where we stopped for the night. Mr Archer enquired at three inns before he found one with two rooms free, and a space for Langton in a shared room in the attics. Lady Isabella insisted I share the bed with her, rather than use some blankets on the floor, but I don't think either of us slept much. The bed was comfortable enough, and I was used to sharing, but I couldn't help thinking that Lord Marstone must have sent someone after us by now.

We found out that he had the next morning, at the second place we stopped to change horses. Langton hadn't talked—again—but the silence didn't feel as uncomfortable this morning. Perhaps I was getting used to it. When we pulled into the inn yard, he jumped down and spoke to Mr Archer, who went into the inn. Mr Archer was frowning when he came out, and said something to Langton before going to speak to the post boys. Then he climbed in and we set off.

"Is something wrong?" I asked, half expecting Langton to ignore me.

"Marstone's man is ahead of us."

"Ahead? How do you know?"

"Archer asked if the innkeeper had seen a young lady with a maid and a manservant. He said no, but that someone else asked exactly that an hour ago."

That was a good idea—had Langton suggested it to Mr Archer? "Why are we going on, then? Won't Lord Marstone's man realise he must be ahead of us and just wait?"

"We're going by a different route now, and we're going faster than we managed yesterday." He looked at me, and actually smiled. "Bringing Fletcher and Billy along was a good idea, Moll. If that man comes back and asks again, he still won't be any the wiser."

Good heavens—praise from Langton!

"We're going by Andover and Salisbury instead of Bath," he added. That didn't mean anything to me—I'd never heard of those places, let alone knew where they were or how far off. But I wasn't going to display my ignorance and spoil the warm feeling Langton's approval had caused. Perhaps he wasn't so bad after all.

That warm feeling soon wore off. Not because of anything Langton said—for a change. It was because now I knew someone *was* looking for us.

"Moll?"

"What?"

"How *did* Fletcher come to have a bast— baby?"

"Why are you asking now?"

He seemed a little red about the face, but that might have been the breeze. "Lady Jesson gave her a position, and she seems… I mean, a proper lady wouldn't employ…"

"A fallen woman?"

"Er, yes."

"That's Sarah's story to tell—if she wants anyone else to know."

"Did her… the man refuse to marry her after…?"

I suppose that happened to some women. Brides with big bellies weren't exactly unknown in Over Minster, and few were bothered by it. Ma had said it was foolish, though, to risk a babe not having a father—faithless swains were possible, but so were men having accidents or sudden fevers.

"The man didn't promise anything at all. Nor even ask." Let him make of that what he would.

"But didn't her—?"

"It's Sarah's story."

He pressed his lips together for a moment, but then nodded, and I let him sit and work it out for himself.

Langton's silence gave me more time to worry about getting caught. I knew the person asking had taken a different road, but Lord

Marstone, or his man of business, must know there was more than one way to Lord Wingrave's place in Devonshire. What would Lord Marstone do to us if we were caught before we got there? And could Lady Wingrave protect us if Lord Wingrave was still out of the country?

My fears made me suspicious of every rider who passed us and every vehicle that tried to overtake. After a while though, when nobody took any interest in us, I became less nervous. Until, after we'd changed horses a couple of times, a rider approaching from behind didn't overtake. I turned to look more closely, and my movement alerted Langton.

"It's Mr Carterton," he said, and my stomach unknotted itself. Well, not completely—if Mr Carterton had caught up with us, there was no reason why Lord Marstone's men could not.

"Stop the carriage," Langton called to the postboys, and they guided the horses over to the edge of the road. The chaise door opened, and my lady got out, her face white.

"It's only Mr Carterton, my lady," I called.

She leaned on the carriage and closed her eyes—in relief, I hoped. I was about to climb down, but Mr Carterton had come up by then, and dismounted beside her.

He said something to her, then Mr Archer got out. After they talked, Mr Archer called to the postboys to carry on to Salisbury, and Mr Carterton mounted up again and followed behind.

Mr Carterton bespoke a private parlour in the inn in Salisbury, and escorted my lady in before going off again to talk to the innkeeper. He wasn't any better dressed than Mr Archer, but the nice way he spoke must have told the innkeeper he was quality, for he got much faster service than we'd had at any of the places we'd stopped before.

I sat down with Sarah and Billy at one of the tables, and my lady sat at another, and it wasn't long before a couple of waiters arrived with trays of food.

"This looks good," Sarah said, bouncing Billy on her knee as I served slices of chicken pie and heaps of vegetables from the dishes before us. My lady had similar fare on her table, but ignored it.

"It does." The smell was making my stomach rumble. "Do you want me to hold Billy while you cut up your pie?" She would be able to eat one-handed, then.

Mr Carterton came into the parlour as we were eating, and threw his coat over the back of a chair at Lady Isabella's table. "Archer is arranging for a second post-chaise," he said, loud enough for us to hear. "We'll travel faster that way. May I join you?"

I saw his expression as he asked—as if he was worried about her. She nodded, and he sat and served himself from the dishes in the centre of the table. She toyed with her food while he ate. I couldn't hear what they said, but I could see the way she looked at him, and blushed and lowered her eyes. It wasn't quite the dreamy look she'd had over Fancy Man, but I thought she might be getting there. Men didn't blush like girls, but there was something in Mr Carterton's face that said he liked her in that way, too. I wondered if he really was courting someone else, as Lady Isabella thought. He would make a good husband for her—it was a pity her father hadn't chosen him.

Sarah was watching them with the same speculation, but we didn't speak about it. Instead, I asked her if she'd been this way before. She hadn't, but she did describe travelling to the north of England with Lady Milton and her husband, and about the wild hills and moors around their estates. I'd be interested to see places like that, but not to live there—it didn't sound nearly as exciting as London.

The door opened and banged into a chest against the wall, and my fork clattered onto the plate. Two men—large men—came in and stood beside the door. Their boots and breeches were covered in mud splashes. Lord Marstone's men—they must be. Who else would come barging in like that?

Mr Carterton jumped up. "This is a private parlour. Take yourselves off." His hands curled into fists.

Billy's face crumpled up at the raised voice, and Sarah bounced him again, giving him his wooden teething stick to suck. The men took no notice, and only moved aside a little to allow another man in.

He wasn't as large as the first two, but it was easy to see he was in charge. Behind him, another man gripped Langton by the arm. Langton looked a bit dishevelled, and I hoped he hadn't got hurt trying to escape.

"You must be Carterton," the man in charge said, then looked at my lady. "Lady Isabella, your father has sent me to fetch you home."

"Who the devil are you?" Mr Carterton asked. I thought he was going to try fighting—but there was only him and Langton, and four of them. Fancy Man would have tried, no doubt, and been thoroughly beaten for his efforts. Mr Carterton had more sense.

"The name's Jasperson, from Bow Street. I have a warrant for your arrest on a charge of kidnapping, along with your accomplices."

Kidnapping? Accomplices?

"I did nothing of the sort, I assure you," Mr Carterton said. "I am merely escorting—"

"You set out after her, didn't you?" Jasperson said. "That's what a footman at your father's house told Lord Marstone's man."

I suppose Mr Carterton hadn't kept his journey secret from his servants.

"And she's run off from home. The ostlers said you…"

Where was Mr Archer? Did he know these men were here?

"…all arrived on the London road. If you ain't kidnapping her now, you should be taking her in the opposite direction."

"Mr Jasperson!" Lady Isabella raised her voice. Everyone's attention was on her—I took my chance and leaned towards Sarah.

"Make Billy cry."

She frowned.

"If he makes enough noise they'll send you out. Warn Mr Archer."

She finally understood and pulled the teething stick from her son's mouth. He gaped for a moment, then began to cry.

"I left London of my own free will," Lady Isabella was saying. "The others cannot be…"

No-one was taking any notice of the baby's noise. "Sorry, Billy," I whispered, and gave his arm a hard pinch. That might lose me Sarah's friendship, but she wouldn't enjoy being arrested, either.

"...accomplices, as no crime has—"

Billy's screams were louder than my lady's voice, and Jasperson turned towards us.

"Better take him outside, Mrs Fletcher." I was almost shouting above Billy's furious protests. "*If* that's all right with you, Mr Jasperson?"

Jasperson jerked his head towards the door, and Sarah hurried out. The man holding Langton moved aside for her to leave, then thrust Langton into the room and closed the door. Sarah walked past the window, Billy still waving his fists and screaming.

Langton sat in Sarah's chair. "You all right, Moll?" he whispered.

"So far." I was pleased he'd asked.

Mr Carterton was still arguing with Jasperson, but he didn't get anywhere.

"She's a minor, sir," Jasperson said. "The law considers she don't know what's best for her. I'm only doing what his lordship says."

Bloody men!

"Did you find us by chance?" Mr Carterton asked.

Did it matter how we'd been found?

"Aye," the runner said. "His lordship sent his man off on the Bath road, but there's many ways you could have got to Devonshire. Seemed to make sense to get to within a few miles of your destination and arrest you there. When we stopped here to change horses, one of Marstone's men recognised Langton. Can't say I'm sorry; it's saved us all a couple of days."

That was clever.

"Which one of Marstone's men?" I asked Langton.

"Barlow." He almost spat the word out.

Langton's friend. Or perhaps his former friend, now? This wasn't the time to ask.

Jasperson allowed us to finish our meal before his men escorted us out, but I'd lost my appetite. Lady Isabella would be forced to marry someone she didn't want, and I was likely to get arrested. Langton, too. Jasperson hadn't said so, but Lord Marstone was just the type to make everyone's live as miserable as possible.

When we got outside, the chaise we'd come in was waiting ready, along with a much shabbier one.

"Where's the woman with the brat?" one of Jasperson's men asked.

Jasperson shrugged. "Not our business. We was only hired to return Lady Isabella and her servants."

Barlow appeared from behind the shabby chaise, with an unpleasant grin of triumph in my direction. There was a sudden scuffle behind me, and Langton shot past. Barlow tried to get away, but he wasn't fast enough and Langton landed a fist in his face before two of Jasperson's men pulled him off.

"Tie his hands, lads," Jasperson said as he herded me and my lady to our chaise. "Don't want him trying that again. You, Barlow, you get up behind this one."

We set off before the others, and the last I saw of Langton was one of Jasperson's men winding a bit of rope around his wrists as another escorted Mr Carterton into the second carriage.

CHAPTER 15

My lady didn't say anything for some time. She was looking out of the window, but her eyes never fixed on anything, so I don't think she was really seeing the villages and fields we'd passed going the other way. Poor lady.

Poor Langton, too, and poor me, if Lord Marstone did have us arrested.

Jasperson had talked about kidnapping. I didn't know, but I guessed that kidnapping an earl's daughter would be a hanging matter. Until we'd set off for Devonshire, I'd never really believed that anything worse than losing my position might happen to me. All the worry about being overtaken, and now this—it was too much, and I gulped, trying not to cry.

"Don't worry, Molly." Lady Isabella squeezed my hand. "My father won't want this to go before a judge. That would cause too much gossip. And Mr Carterton's father is a baron."

"He'll be all right, then." I sniffed, and felt in my coat pockets for a handkerchief.

"He'll help you and Langton, too." She sounded very sure, and I tried my best to believe her. "You did very well to get Sarah and Billy away."

"Mr Archer will take her back to London, won't he?" At least she might get out of this unscathed.

"Yes, of course. He's Will's man, and Will would definitely look after anyone who'd tried to help me." She sounded like she wasn't worried about herself or us, but she was holding her own handkerchief so hard her knuckles were white.

I blew my nose, feeling a little better. "What will happen to Sarah?" I didn't want to be worrying all the way back to London, and talking might help my lady to cheer up a little, too.

"Jasperson wasn't interested in—"

"I meant when she's finished Lady Jesson's new wardrobe."

"I suppose she might get another position as a seamstress if she can find a decent woman to leave Billy with."

I'd already told my lady about the wet nurse who was looking after the babe. "It would cost a lot more to leave Billy with Mrs Leggett than it did at that horrible place in St Giles."

"It all comes down to money, doesn't it?' My lady sighed. "Or power and influence, in my father's case. If I had some money…"

"If you had the money, my lady, you could set her up in her own business. She's good enough, and she'd be a fair employer, too, I reckon. Not like that Madame Donnard."

She gazed out of the window again, but she was thinking this time. "I'll try, Molly. Whatever happens to me, I'll be able to get word to Will when he returns. You'll explain to him, won't you, if I cannot?"

"Of course, my lady." If I wasn't in gaol.

"What else will she need? Your mother was a seamstress, wasn't she?"

"Yes, my lady. She'd need customers, for a start."

"Lady Jesson… Oh, I know she'll have her new wardrobe by then, but she can put the word around. And premises…"

Planning Sarah's new life got us a couple of hours on our way. We stopped for the usual changes, and Jasperson didn't make a fuss when I told him my lady needed to use the necessary. Jasperson kept Barlow by the chaise whenever we got out, which I was glad of.

We didn't stop when it went dark, even though the moon was

often behind a cloud. We probably made better time with hardly anyone else on the roads. Jasperson even allowed us to stop for breakfast as it got light. It was a relief to stretch our legs—and backs and necks, after trying to sleep leaning against the sides of the chaise.

It was late in the morning when we finally arrived back outside Marstone House. Jasperson's chaise pulled up, and ours came to a stop behind it. Barlow jumped down and went to knock at the front door before Jasperson reached our chaise and handed my lady down.

I looked at the other carriage, but Mr Carterton didn't get out, and the man next to Langton on the outside seat had his hand on Langton's collar. Then we were inside, and Mowbray closed the door behind us.

I was happy not to have been arrested, but Lord Marstone could still order that. And Jasperson had taken Langton off wherever he was taking Mr Carterton, so he wasn't safe yet, either.

Barlow leered at me from behind Mowbray, and I was pleased to see one eye beginning to swell up from where Langton had hit him. Mowbray turned and told him to go and get clean and into his livery, sharpish. Not everyone likes a snitch, and it seemed that Mowbray was one such person. Not that it would do me or my lady much good.

Mowbray turned to Lady Isabella. "His lordship instructed that you be taken to him as soon as you arrived, my lady. Follow me."

She raised her chin. "I will have a bath and a rest first. See that hot water is sent to my room." She set off up the stairs without waiting for Mowbray to reply, and I followed.

"My lady," Mowbray pleaded, hurrying after us. "His lordship was most insistent. He is not well. His physician insists that he not be agitated."

He hadn't been well before—he'd probably lost his temper again when he was told my lady was missing, and made himself worse. I tried very hard not to feel pleased about it.

My lady stopped suddenly, and turned around. "Then do not tell him I have arrived. If you tell him I am here and have refused to see him, then it is *you* who will be agitating him." She glared at the butler until he nodded. "Hot water?"

"Yes, my lady."

He bowed and went back down the stairs. I'd never seen Lady Isabella like that with the servants before, but facing down Mowbray wasn't going to make any difference, more's the pity.

"You'll feel more the thing after a bath, my lady," I said, leaving my bonnet and coat in the dressing room and readying some towels.

The knock on the door was Lady Cerney, not the hot water, so I busied myself in the dressing room while the two ladies talked. But I left the door open.

"Bella, I'm sorry to see you back here. I never thought Marstone would go so far as to set the law on you and Carterton."

"Aunt, the runner said he had a warrant to arrest Mr Carterton. How did Papa even know Mr Carterton might come after us?"

I put down the fresh gown I was readying for my lady and stepped closer to the door.

"He called the morning you left," Lady Cerney said. "I told him you were heading for Wingrave's place. I can only assume we were overheard..."

Barlow. Must have been.

"...but why Marstone accused him of kidnapping, I've no idea. It was clear you'd run away long before Carterton arrived. Isabella, why didn't you tell me Carterton was... interested in you? My brother might have accepted—"

"He's not," Bella said.

I wasn't so sure about that. I'd seen the way he looked at her in that inn in Salisbury.

"A pity... I think he would have made a good husband."

The hot water arrived then, and I supervised O'Connor and one of the temporary footmen setting the bath out and filling it. Not Barlow, to my relief.

Lady Cerney said something more before she left, but I couldn't hear it over the noise the footmen were making. I asked my lady if she wanted anything to eat, but she didn't. When she was bathed and dressed she went to see her father. I went in search of more food—

although we'd stopped for breakfast, that was hours ago and I was hungry again.

One of the kitchen maids got me some fresh bread and cold meat, and made tea, and I sat at one end of the table in the servants' hall. Barlow came in not long after, shaved and in his full livery.

"Messed up your position here, Moll," he said, coming to sit beside me. "Be lucky if you keep your job." He moved his chair closer. Too close.

"Gave you thirty pieces of silver, did they?"

He frowned, not understanding. He probably hadn't paid attention in church.

"I thought Jem Langton was your friend. You've got him arrested for kidnapping—when you know it was no such thing." I pushed my plate away, having no appetite now for the rest.

He had the grace to look ashamed, but only for a moment. "He should have thought of that before he helped Lady Isabella run off. Anyway, I'm not too sorry he's out of the way." He put one hand on my knee.

I clenched my fists to stop myself slapping him, then had a better idea. The teapot was half-full and the tea still hot, and Barlow leapt up with a yell as the liquid hit him in the chest. It soaked in wonderfully well, turning his neckcloth a delicate shade of brown. It didn't show so much on his coat, apart from the tea leaves stuck to the fabric, but the mark would be there when it dried. I hoped the water that reached his breeches had been hot enough to hurt.

"You bitch!"

I ducked just in time, and the fist he swung at my face grazed the top of my head. My cap and hair softened the blow, and by the time he'd drawn his arm back for another try, O'Connor had pulled him back. I was lucky O'Connor had been near enough to come running. Tipping the tea onto Barlow might not have been one of my better ideas.

"What is going on here?" Mowbray demanded, making shooing motions at the gawping maids and the boot boy.

"That bitch threw—"

"You will moderate your language, Barlow!" Mowbray thundered —I didn't know he had it in him. "Simons?"

"I spilled the tea on him, Mr Mowbray, when he put his hand on my leg."

"She led me on!"

"I did not."

Mowbray rubbed a hand across his forehead, suddenly looking old and tired. "Barlow, go and change, and get your coat cleaned. I will decide later who pays for the damage if the tea stain will not come out."

O'Connor let go of him, and he stamped off after one vicious look at me.

"If you please, Mr Mowbray…" Sally spoke up. "Molly didn't lead him on at all. Barlow's always puttin' his hands where they're not wanted." A murmur from the other women around backed her up.

Mowbray sighed, but didn't look at all surprised at Sally's words. "Stay away from him, Simons, if you can."

"I can't if he gets sent to my lady's room, Mr Mowbray."

He rubbed his forehead again. "I'll make sure he is not. Get on with your work, the rest of you. Simons, a word…" He waited until the other staff had gone about their business, then spoke in a low voice. "His lordship ordered me to ensure you do not leave the house. Will you give me your word, Molly, or must I have you locked in your room?"

I couldn't leave my lady. "I promise."

"Good, good. The same goes for Lady Isabella. Do I need to station a footman outside her door to ensure that?"

"Where would she go?"

"Hmm. Very well. Now, best you are not here when Barlow returns, eh?"

Wonderful. Barlow put his hands where they're not wanted, and it was *me* who had to stay out of *his* way.

I went back up to my lady's room, and busied myself brushing down the clothes she'd been wearing and putting them away. It didn't seem as if she'd have any further use for a maid's gown. Nor for the rest of her fine things, if she was to be taken back to Marstone Park.

She didn't look too happy when she returned and slumped into a chair by the window, but she didn't look desperate, either.

"My father wants me to marry Mr Carterton."

"That's good, isn't it, my lady? Better than Lord Narwood." Better than Fancy Man, too. "Did he say what Jasperson did with Mr Carterton?" And Langton.

"They were taken to Bow Street. Father threatened to have... have them prosecuted for kidnapping if I did not agree to the match."

"I thought you said he wouldn't do that? Too much gossip."

"I'm sure Lord Carterton will get his son released quickly. But if he does have you two charged with—"

You two? "Me, my lady?"

She sighed. "Yes, he was threatening to have you both before a magistrate for kidnapping. But don't worry—I agreed to the match."

"I..." I felt I ought to say it would be better for her if she hadn't agreed, even if that got me in trouble. If her father had still been insisting on Lord Narwood, I might have summoned up the courage to say so and trusted Mr Carterton or Lord Wingrave to get me released. But Mr Carterton was a good man—probably better than anyone else Lord Marstone might pick. "Thank you, my lady. Do you wish for some refreshment now?"

"If you please."

Below stairs, Barlow was trying to wheedle the laundrywoman into leaving her other work to get the tea stains out of his livery coat. I was tempted to listen, for she was nearly as old as Ma and wasn't putting up with any demands from the likes of Barlow. But I didn't want him to spot me, so I hurried on towards the kitchen.

"Jem!"

Langton was sitting at one end of the table with a mug of ale and a plate of bread, meat, and cheese before him. He looked grubby and tired, but smiled when he saw me. A lovely smile, it was, not the polite one he had been using recently.

"Hello, Moll."

"Oh, I'm glad you're safe."

"Me, too. Mr Carterton's father arranged a paper from the magistrate to make Jasperson let him out, and he insisted that it applied to me, too." He grimaced. "I'm not out of the suds yet, though. Jasperson only agreed if I got sent back here. Mowbray's got orders to lock me up."

I looked around—apart from Barlow's voice still floating in from the laundry room, there weren't any other men about to guard him.

"After I've eaten," Langton added. "I think he's being lenient because it cannot be many more months until Lord Wingrave takes over. He's got his eye on the future."

Like you. I didn't say it, though. We'd argued enough on the coach, and he *had* helped my lady.

"Do you know what happened to Sarah?"

"Archer came to see Mr Carterton. He said... I mean, Mr Carterton said that Lady Isabella would want to know that Fletcher was safe. Archer had to ride on ahead, so he gave her the fare for the stage. She should be back with Lady Jesson by now, or later today. Depends when the coaches run."

"Oh, that's good." As long as nothing happened to her on the way. But I didn't see that Mr Archer had much choice.

"She'll be all right, Moll, you'll see."

This friendly Jem was a much nicer person than the one of the last few weeks, and he'd even managed to say Sarah's name without sneering or scowling.

Mr Carterton called later that afternoon, and agreed to the match. Lord Marstone had already arranged a special licence, and Lady Isabella was to be married the next day at eleven o'clock.

My lady seemed resigned to it. I laid out some of her gowns on the bed, and she considered them carefully, as if it mattered that she looked well for her bridegroom. "The cream one, I think."

"That's a good choice, my lady." It was intended as a ball gown, but it was one she hadn't worn before. I was happy that she was making the best of the situation—for her sake, and for Mr Carterton. "There's some roses out in the garden—shall I make you a posy? They'll go lovely with that gown."

"Yes, please."

She dismissed me then, and I decided to cut the roses right away, in case it was raining in the morning. I started by asking Mr Mowbray—he'd been decent to me and to Jem, so it was best to ask his permission before I left the house even if it was only to go into the garden.

But I went out to the stables first, and gave one of the grooms a sixpence to fetch Sprout for me. Sprout got another sixpence to go to Lady Jesson's house and let me know when Sarah was back safe. I was making good use of Mr Archer's money.

As I cut a handful of roses and some buds that would go nicely in my lady's hair, I wondered if I should have been packing up my lady's garments. She would be removing to Mr Carterton's house when she was married, or to Lord Carterton's country estate in Sussex. That was the other side of London from Marstone Park, my lady explained when I asked her.

No matter, packing up would be a quick job with Tamworth's help. Then it finally dawned on me that I would be going with her. Just when I was in more sympathy with Jem, and he was beginning to be friendly towards me.

CHAPTER 16

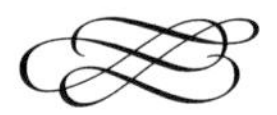

My lady was ready in plenty of time for her wedding the next morning, but eleven o'clock passed and no-one came to summon her to Lord Marstone's room. After pacing up and down for more than half an hour, she sent me downstairs to find out what was happening.

"We're waiting for the priest to arrive," Mowbray said. "Mr Carterton is in the library."

I went to let my lady know, then sat on the top step of the main staircase—*not* something any servant should do, but it was the best place to listen for the priest's arrival.

He came at last, and Mowbray escorted him up the stairs. I leaned as far over the bannisters as I dared, but I could only make out the top of a grey wig above a black coat, and the way his hand kept going to fiddle with the bands at his throat. Mowbray glanced upwards as he ushered the priest into the corridor below me.

"Shall I bring my lady?" I called, but not too loudly.

He nodded.

Lady Isabella was sitting in her usual window seat, her hands gripped together in her lap. She stood as soon as I entered, her hands clenched at her sides.

"He's a good man, my lady."

"I know." Her smile was rather sad. "But it would have been better for him to have had a choice."

"The priest is here."

She nodded, and I followed her along the corridor to the stairs. Lady Cerney was waiting with Mowbray on the floor below, and Lady Isabella went with her towards Lord Marstone's room, then Mowbray escorted Mr Carterton in.

Mowbray retreated no further than the top of the stairs, and I crept down far enough to see along that corridor. Tamworth and Mrs Wardle were standing together in the doorway to Lady Cerney's room; beyond them, several of the maids and a couple of footmen were trying to be inconspicuous. They were all looking along the corridor to Lord Marstone's room, even though the door was closed.

How long did it take to read the marriage service? I'd sat through quite a few in Over Minster, but this priest might make it shorter as his lordship was so ill.

I was just thinking that the deed might be done by now when the knocker on the front door pounded, the sound echoing from the marble floor and walls. A quick murmur of voices, one raised in protest—Barlow? Then I heard hurried footsteps and a gentleman ran up the stairs towards us, with a still-protesting Barlow behind him.

"My lord!" Mowbray exclaimed. The gentleman was known to Mowbray, then. And his face bore a distinct resemblance to my lady's.

"Where's Bella?"

Mowbray stepped forward. "My lord, you cannot—"

"In Lord Marstone's room, being married." I pointed down the corridor. "Third door on the left."

He strode down the corridor, Mowbray and Barlow hurrying after him.

"My lord, you cannot—"

"Stand aside, Mowbray." And Lord Wingrave—for it could be no-one else—pushed the door open.

Mowbray waved Barlow away, and the pair of them returned to the head of the stairs. Nothing happened for a few minutes, then Lord

Wingrave came out of the bedroom with Lady Isabella, one arm around her shoulders. Was my lady married, or not? I couldn't tell from her expression. If she wasn't, then I wouldn't be leaving Marstone House, and Jem, just yet. I hoped for her sake and mine that she wasn't.

Lord Wingrave glared up the corridor as he escorted his sister downstairs, and everyone scattered, including me. As my lady didn't need me, I went down to the servants' hall. It wasn't time for our dinner yet, but Cook had made pots of tea anyway, and it looked like most of the servants were sitting around the large table talking. Except Mowbray and Mrs Wardle, but I wouldn't be surprised if they were gossiping just as much, somewhere out of sight of the rest of us.

I took a vacant place and someone pushed a full cup towards me. Barlow, at the far end, wasn't looking nearly so pleased with himself now—and no wonder.

"…hasn't set foot in the house for years…"

"…doesn't look a day older then when his lordship made him get married."

"…if the old lord hasn't stuck his spoon in the wall yet, this'll see him…"

They were interested in Lord Wingrave, not Lady Isabella. I shouldn't have been surprised. *I* cared what happened to my lady, but Lord Wingrave would be their next employer.

"He walked in like he owns the place," Barlow muttered.

"He soon will," one of the maids put in. "From what I've seen, his lordship's in a bad way." The smile she sent in Barlow's direction was gleeful, and I guessed that Barlow had bothered her, too.

"Lord Marstone isn't dead yet." Barlow's voice was louder this time. "His orders that Lord Wingrave is not to enter the house are still in place. Mowbray shouldn't have let him in."

"*You* let him in," I pointed out. "What was Mowbray supposed to do? Stop him by force, when a fine, upstanding lad like you couldn't?" There were sniggers all round. "Or didn't dare? Didn't want your other eye blackening?"

It was petty of me to poke at him like that, but oh, it did feel good!

A touch on my shoulder distracted me from his reply. It was the youngest scullery maid. "If you please, Miss Simons, there's a lad outside says he must see you."

"Lad?"

"Right scruffy. He wouldn't go away."

Sprout?

"I'll get rid of him. Here, have my place."

"Miss Fletcher's back," Sprout said, as soon as I stepped out of the back door. "I asked fer the girl to fetch that footman, but she said 'e was locked up." His eyes were round, his cap in his hands and his hair plastered to his head by the rain.

Now Lord Wingrave was here, would he release Jem?

"Thank you for finding out about Sarah. But why did you want Langton? Is there a message?"

"No, miss. There's... I mean..." He looked down at his feet.

I stepped outside and drew him away from the door—the house kept the worst of the rain off.

"Well?"

"Jonno's my friend, I don't wan' ter blab, but... but someone should know."

"What do you think I'm going to do—arrest Jonno?"

Sprout shook his head.

"What's he done?"

"Spyin' on the 'ouse, miss."

"Like you've been?"

He stood up straighter at that. "No! I've been waitin' to see if I can be of service."

I suppose it wasn't quite the same. "Who's he working for?"

"Don't know 'is name, but I've seen 'im before. Forriner, 'e is—'e don't speak quite like the normal ladies and gents."

Fancy Man? The Spanish spy—what did he want with my lady?

"Go on."

"I didn't reckon Jonno was doin' no 'arm just watchin'. But 'e got one o' the maids to meet the cove in the alley yesterday." He jerked his head in the direction of the mews. "She's out there wiv 'im again now."

Who had been missing from the servants' hall? Tamworth was too old for someone like Fancy Man to try flirting with. Sally? She'd flirt all right, but I didn't think she'd do anything stupid.

"About my age? Black hair?"

He nodded. Sally, then. But a man who'd been trying to court Lady Isabella wouldn't pay a street boy to set up a flirtation. He must be using Sally to try to get to my lady.

"Thank you, Sprout. If… if the foreign gentleman does… tries…" What? Kidnapping?

"I'll 'ang around, miss, and raise a cry if I see anyfink wrong." He slapped his cap back on his head and crept off, using bushes and the bits of hedge to stay out of sight as much as possible.

I had to find out where Lady Isabella was. O'Connor was slouching in the porter's chair in the front hall.

"Have you seen Lady Isabella?"

He sat up. "Got me in trouble, you did, Moll. You and Lady Isabella." He didn't sound angry, though. Just grumpy.

"How so?"

"The night you left, Langton wasn't outside my lady's door when I went to take over. I thought he'd gone off to the privy, so I didn't say anything. They'd have found out a lot sooner if I had."

"It didn't make any difference in the end, did it? Besides, it's only Barlow who likes getting other folks into trouble."

He grinned. "Heh. I'll bet he's glad Lord Wingrave's back, to find out how he helped his sister get caught."

"What did he do?"

"Overheard Lady Cerney telling Mr Carterton that you were on your way to Devonshire, he did, and then went straight to his lordship. And *volunteered* to go along because he could identify you and Langton."

I'd guessed it must have been something like that. But I'd chatted too long. "What's happening? Where are the family?"

"Lady Isabella went into the parlour, then Lord Wingrave came down and went in to see her. Mowbray put Mr Carterton in the library—Lord Wingrave's with him now, sure."

"Is Lady Isabella still in the parlour?"

"She is. Mowbray just took some tea in."

My lady hadn't rung for me, but it would do no harm to put my head into the parlour to see if she needed anything else.

She wasn't there, but the tea things were still on the table, with a half-drunk cup of tea. Bother—I shouldn't have wasted time talking to O'Connor.

Sally wouldn't dare bring Fancy Man into the house, so she must have got Lady Isabella to go outside. I turned and hurried back through the baize door and down the corridor to the below-stairs exit to the garden. No-one noticed my haste—they were all too busy gossiping.

It was still raining, but there was no help for it—I stepped out into the garden. Sprout might know something.

I didn't get that far—there was a black umbrella showing above the bushes near the summer house. Creeping closer, I spotted Sally beneath it, watching my lady and Fancy Man inside the building. They were sitting apart, and my panic subsided a little—no-one had done anything stupid yet.

While I was trying to think what to do next, Mr Carterton came striding towards the summer house. He had his jaw clenched and his hands in fists—I wouldn't like to be in Fancy Man's shoes right now.

He sent Sally away, and I followed her into the house—there was no sense in me staying outside to watch any longer, not with the rain. Mr Carterton would make sure my lady was safe.

Once inside, I brushed the worst of the wet off my gown and went to find O'Connor again. "Where's Lord Wingrave now?"

"Library."

"Anyone with him?"

He shook his head, and I went and tapped on the library door.

"Come!"

Lord Wingrave sat in one of the armchairs near the window, a glass of something red in one hand. "Yes, what is it?" He looked tired, and sounded impatient.

"If you please, my lord, I'm Lady Isabella's maid, and—"

"Molly Simons?"

My mouth fell open at him knowing my name.

He sat up straight and put his glass on a nearby table. "Bell—That is, Lady Isabella has told me something of you, and how you helped her. You have my thanks, as well as hers."

I felt my face going red, and bobbed a curtsey.

"You did well," he said. "I will talk to you later, about everything that has happened, but not now."

"Yes, my lord. I just wished to ask you… The footman who came with us—Lord Marstone ordered him to be locked up."

"Langton?"

His knowledge didn't surprise me this time. "Yes, my lord."

"Tell Mowbray to let him out, on my authority. And neither of you will leave the house, if you please."

I tried to hide my grimace, but didn't quite manage it.

"This is not an imprisonment, Molly." He smiled, looking ever so much like my lady as he did. "As I said, I wish to talk to you both, and I have many other things to do."

"Sorry, my lord." I curtseyed and left before I could embarrass myself any further.

Mowbray had the grace to look guilty when I went to him, and gave me the key. "Last door before the wine cellar," he said.

Poor Jem—those rooms didn't even have windows. But when I found the right door and turned the key, it didn't seem as bad as I'd thought. Boxes and empty trunks were stacked up against one wall, leaving just enough space for a pallet on the floor. Jem sat on it with his back against the wall and legs stretched out before him. A lantern gave plenty of light for reading the book in his hands.

"Hello Molly." There was that friendly smile again. "Did they let you bring my dinner?"

"I've come to let you out. Lord Wingrave's back, and gave me permission to."

He dropped the book and scrambled to his feet. "Lord Wingrave? *In* the house?"

"Came right in, he did. Pushed past Barlow and went straight into his lordship's room, where Lady Isabella was getting married."

"Taken charge, has he? Good." He was folding his blankets as he spoke, along with the clean shirt draped over a nearby box. "Who's Lady Isabella married to?"

"I'm not sure if she's married or not—but if she is, it's to Mr Carterton."

"Oh, well. He seems like a decent man. Can you bring the lantern?"

There were fewer people in the servants' hall when we walked past the door, but I could hear Barlow complaining about something. Jem heard him, too. He dropped the things in his arms and strode in, not stopping to reply to questions about how he had got out but heading straight for Barlow.

Barlow must have seen violence in Jem's face, for he stood up so quickly his chair fell over. "Got a message to take," he gabbled, and fairly ran out of the far door. Jem sprinted after him.

"Jem!"

My shriek made him pause, and he turned to face me—and the rest of his audience, all gaping at him. His hands unclenched slowly. "I'll get him yet," he muttered, as he went to pick up his things again.

"Yes, but not here, in the house." I lowered my voice as he got closer to me. "You don't want to spoil all your efforts to be in Lord Wingrave's favour by brawling here."

He let out a breath. "True."

"And Lord Wingrave said you and I were not to leave the house. He wants to talk to us when he has a moment."

Jem frowned.

"We're not in trouble—he thanked me for helping my lady."

"That's good. I *will* get even with Barlow, though." He set off up the back stairs. I followed, for I'd had an idea.

"It would be unfortunate, wouldn't it, if Barlow happened to get involved in a taproom brawl? Once Lord Wingrave has spoken to you, of course."

"Hmm."

"Lady Isabella could send you out on an errand when it's Barlow's day off."

"How would I know—?"

"Sprout'll follow him if you give him some coin."

He stopped and looked at me. "That lad'll be rich by the time we've finished." Then he grinned and winked at me. "You know, you're not just a pretty face, Moll!"

I stood there while he carried on, the sound of his footsteps fading. He thought I was pretty?

CHAPTER 17

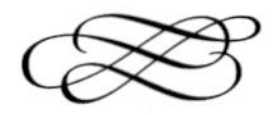

I didn't find out what had happened with Lady Isabella until later that afternoon. O'Connor told me that Mr Carterton and my lady had gone into the library with Fancy Man, and a bit later Lord Wingrave and Fancy Man had left the house. Lady Isabella hadn't rung for me, so I asked Mrs Wardle if I might sit in her room and practise my reading. Puzzling out the long words kept my curiosity under control. Mostly.

At last Lady Isabella rang for me. I found her pacing up and down her room again, and my heart sank until I saw the smile on her face. I think it was the first time I'd ever seen her look truly happy.

"Oh, Molly! Everything has turned out so well! I am betrothed to Mr Carterton."

"What happened, my lady?" She'd been betrothed to him that morning, and it hadn't brought her any joy then. "All I know is that Lord Wingrave is here and taking charge. Did you not get married this morning?"

She finally sat down, and gestured for me to do so, too. "Will arrived just as the priest was saying the words..."

So she *was* married?

"…but then it turned out that Nick… Mr Carterton… had diverted the real priest and sent his butler along to pretend."

His butler? "Mr Carterton did that?"

She giggled. "I know, he seemed too…"

"Sensible?"

"Yes, sensible. Sensible is good in a husband, I know, but not *all* the time!"

"So you would not have been married even if Lord Wingrave hadn't come?" And we would not be leaving Marstone House just yet.

"No. Father would have found out soon enough, I suppose, but Nick did it to make enough time for Will to get here."

If Mr Carterton had gone to those lengths to make sure they weren't married, why was she so happy now?

"What did Fancy— I mean, why was Senhor da Gama here?"

"He came to warn me—to ask me to warn Will—about his orders to assassinate someone, and then he was jealous when he found us together."

I was really confused by now. Who was jealous?

"I'm not telling this very well, am I?"

"No, my lady. Why don't you start with Senhor da Gama?"

It took some time, but it turned out that Fancy Man wasn't quite as bad as I'd thought. He *had* been trying to seduce various women, including my lady and Sarah Fletcher's previous mistress, to try to find out government secrets, but hadn't managed to. Lady Isabella had been a target because Lord Wingrave was something to do with the government, although she didn't know what.

But then Senhor da Gama's orders had changed and he was supposed to assassinate some Frenchman coming to talk to our prime minister. He hadn't liked the idea of that, and came to my lady to see if she could make Lord Wingrave listen to him without him being arrested.

"So he's gone now?" I asked. That was the important part.

"Perhaps not yet, but Will did say he'd send him back to Spain. He's just… young and foolish, Molly, really."

A young and foolish spy. Still, I'd gathered that Fancy Man had given my lady some sore-needed confidence when he started to flirt with her, so knowing him hadn't been all bad.

And the story of her betrothal was quite simple in the end. She and Mr Carterton both loved the other, but didn't want the other one to be forced into marriage. Now they'd had some plain talk, they were both happy.

Pity they didn't work that out before my lady ran off.

She was even happier because Lord Wingrave was going to be in charge of everything from now on—Lord Marstone was too ill to give orders, and likely too ill to even notice that Lord Wingrave had moved in. And that meant that her sisters would be able to come for her wedding, with their families, and she would finally get to meet Lady Wingrave.

"We haven't set the date yet," she finished. "It depends when Theresa and Lizzie can get here, but it will be a month or more."

I was summoned to see Lord Wingrave in the library the next morning. In spite of what I'd said to Jem, I was nervous; that first attempt to find Sarah was on my mind.

His lordship looked as if he hadn't slept much, but he was alert enough for all that. "I don't recall seeing you before, Molly. Before yesterday, I mean."

"No, sir. I used to help Betsy—that was the maid the three young ladies shared at Marstone Park. But Betsy went with Lady Elizabeth when she married, and it was just me to look after Lady Isabella after that." That would tell him I'd had no proper training, or experience. "Tamworth—that's Lady Cerney's maid—has been training me up as a proper lady's maid, my lord. I'm learning fast and—"

"Molly, stop!" He held up one hand. "I'm not interviewing you about your future position. That is entirely up to my sister."

Oh—good.

"Tell me about your... excursions into St Giles. Who is the woman you went to find?"

This was the part that could get me into trouble, but I had to tell him. I explained about Fletcher losing her position. "Nothing would satisfy Lady Isabella, my lord, but to find her and help her. I did try to tell her it would be dangerous."

"And yet you accompanied her."

"I couldn't let her go alone, my lord. That fancy man—I mean Senhor da Gama. He went with her, but he was no use at all—more like to have started a fight than help her."

His lips had pursed up. At first I thought he was annoyed with me, but then I realised he was trying not to laugh. I put my chin up. "He insisted he would protect her, my lord, and she believed him. She's only young."

"You are defending her well, Molly. You cannot be much older, though—how are you wiser?"

I found myself telling him about Ma and all the things she'd said, and he listened as if he was really interested. Then he asked for all the details of the two attempts to find Sarah. He nodded now and then while I talked, as if he knew it already. Lady Isabella must have told him something about it, and I wondered if he was checking that I wasn't exaggerating or lying. Although I'd have to be really stupid to risk lying to the likes of him.

"I gather it was your idea to take Billy Fletcher along," he said, when we'd moved on to the escape attempt.

"Yes, my lord."

"That was well done of you. And Bella thinks you had something to do with enabling Fletcher to escape and warn Archer."

"I pinched the baby to make him scream." I wasn't proud of that—poor Billy—but it had worked.

He reached into a drawer of the desk and pulled out a leather purse. It clinked when he put it on the desk in front and pushed it towards me.

"This is something for your pains, Molly." He held up a hand as I was about to speak. "I think you did all you did out of loyalty to your mistress, not for a reward, but you've earned it just the same."

I reached for it—it was as heavy as the one Mr Archer had given me, only a couple of weeks ago, but when I looked inside there was a glint of gold.

"You may count it at your leisure," he went on. "And if you decide to leave my sister's employ at any time, apply to me. I can always find a position for someone quick-witted and loyal. Now, send Langton to me, will you?"

I stood and curtseyed. "Yes, my lord. And thank you."

The physician was called to see Lord Marstone again that afternoon, and orders were given for straw to be laid on the road outside. I'd never heard of that being done, but Tamworth explained that it was common in Town, to deaden the noise of carriages and horses when someone lay dying.

My lady didn't seem too distressed by that news. "I'll miss Will, though," she said, while I was dressing her hair for dinner. "He's going back to Devonshire tomorrow."

With his father at death's door?

Lady Isabella met my eyes in the mirror. "Lady Wingrave is expecting another child, and he's been away for weeks. Our father hasn't *wanted* to speak to him for five years."

Put like that, who could blame him?

"Lady Cerney's staying on for a few weeks. She says she wants to enjoy herself properly without worrying about finding me a suitable husband."

She hadn't worried much about that before, as far as I could tell, but it wouldn't do to say so.

"Will has sent Staverton back to Marstone Park. If Papa becomes lucid enough to want to arrange a different marriage for me, he'll find it difficult without his secretary. And Archer will stay on, in case I need assistance again." She broke off and shrugged.

"How long does... I mean, when..." I stopped. It really wasn't polite to ask when we might be free of the current Lord Marstone, no matter how nicely it was phrased. But my lady understood.

"A week or two, at the most, Smythe thought—that's the physician." She fiddled with the ribbons on the front of her gown. "Molly, I am so grateful for your loyalty. Not many would have risked imprisonment—even if only temporary—to accompany me."

I shrugged, but I was pleased she'd said it. "I didn't know that might happen at the time, my lady." I put the final pin in her hair and stood back to check the overall effect.

"Nevertheless. Is there something I can do for you?"

"Lord Wingrave already gave me some money." It had been fifteen guineas, when I counted it. A year's wages, near enough! I'd resolved to save most of it.

"Perhaps you would like some fabric to make new gowns—*not* hand-me-downs? Sarah Fletcher can help you cut them out."

"I... That would be nice, my lady."

She turned on the stool to face me, and her eyes crinkled at the corners. "Very diplomatic, Molly. That means you have a better idea, but don't like to say so."

I felt my face going hot. "I was just thinking, my lady, that I've never been anywhere outside my village but Marstone Park and the little bit of London around here. And the road to Devonshire, I suppose."

"Neither have I. There are lots of things to see in London, I think. *I* want to see them, too. We will find a guidebook."

"Oh, thank you, my lady. But won't you and Mr Carterton want to go about together?"

"I will ask my aunt, but I think I may still need some kind of chaperone, even though we are now betrothed. Or you may explore on your own—you may have as much time off as you wish. And there must be someone amongst the servants to go with you, if you do not care to go alone."

My face got hot again—Jem knew his way around London.

"...for mourning gowns... Molly, are you listening?"

"Sorry, my lady."

She had that not-quite-laughing look again. "I was saying, I will send you out tomorrow to buy some black fabric and trimming for mourning gowns. I may as well start getting them made."

That might have seemed cold-hearted to some—but I couldn't blame her for it.

I might need to take a footman to carry the parcels.

The sun was shining the next morning as I set out for Bond Street. I wasn't sure how the shopkeepers there would take to a mere maid looking through their goods, but it was too early for proper ladies to be out and about, and I did have a footman in full livery for escort.

All felt good with the world—until Jem opened his mouth when we were halfway there.

"Moll—what really happened that day when Barlow got in trouble with Lady Cerney?"

Back to that again? But at least he was asking. Although I'd insisted at the time that it wasn't my fault, Barlow wouldn't have answered back if it wasn't for him being tripped and dropping the parcels. I didn't want to own up to this new, friendly Jem, but it would be worse if he found out later.

"I paid Sprout to trip him up when he had an armful of parcels." Jem frowned, but I carried on talking before he started to blame me. "But that wasn't what got him into trouble—it was answering back when Lady Cerney told him to pick them up. If he'd just done it, like he should have without being told to, nothing would have come of it."

He stared at me, brows drawn together. "Why, Molly? It's not like you to play tricks like that, is it?"

"I'd had enough of him trying to trap me in corners to have a feel of things he shouldn't."

"Barlow? I've never seen—"

"Yes, *Barlow*," I snapped. "Ask the other maids—I'll bet the whole purse Lord Wingrave gave me that over half of them will say the same."

He considered that for a moment. "Why didn't you say something, if it bothered you so much?"

I stopped, hands on my hips. "Oh, I see. It was my fault that Barlow carried on, was it? Because I didn't complain?"

"Mowbray or Mrs Wardle would have put a stop to it, if they knew. Or Benning and Mrs Williamson at Marstone Park."

"Would they? I say he was forcing his attentions on me, he says I led him on, or I asked him to. Who do they believe? Besides, Mowbray *does* know, and all he did was tell me to stay away from Barlow, as if it was all my fault!"

He didn't answer.

"If I make a fuss, one of us could end up losing our position, and it's easier to replace a maid than half of a matched pair of footmen. Look at what happened to Sarah—Billy wasn't her fault, but it was her who lost her position with Lady Milton." I stepped closer and prodded him in the chest. "*You* assumed she was a… a loose woman, without even bothering to find out what happened. Like you believed Barlow when he said his trouble with Lady Cerney was my fault, because I was jealous. You're the same as all the rest—and then you wonder why women don't always complain."

"You tell 'im, love!" a female voice called, and I looked around to find we had an audience—frowning men and nodding women.

Jem took my arm and pushed through the ring of people, hurrying us along the street. "You were shouting."

I wrenched my arm free. "So? No-one's allowed to—"

"Moll, please. I didn't mean it like that." He hadn't raised his voice —which was quite impressive, when I thought about it later.

"This is the shop." I pushed the door open and went in—he didn't follow. He could wait outside, or go back to Marstone House for all I cared. I'd get things delivered if there was too much for me to carry.

The assistant was gazing at me with round eyes, and I realised I was scowling. I smoothed my face and managed a smile. "I was pestered in the street."

His expression smoothed, but wasn't exactly welcoming. "How may I help you, miss?"

"I am in search of blacks for day dresses and a pelisse for Lord Marstone's daughter. I believe Lady Isabella already has an account with you?"

That worked wonders, and he hurried to fetch bolts of black

bombazine and wool, then lengths of black lace and ribbon. My temper subsided as I concentrated on selecting enough for several gowns and a pelisse. I doubted the black would suit my lady, but that wasn't the point of mourning clothes.

"There you are, miss." The assistant placed the last wrapped parcel on the counter. "Shall I have them delivered, or will your man take them?"

I looked round to see Jem waiting inside the door, wearing his proper footman's face. There were several parcels, and my lips twitched as I recalled Barlow in the street, surrounded by the ones he'd dropped. Jem suddenly looked wary, and I let myself smile.

"Delivered, if you please." Worrying him, even if only for a moment, was revenge enough. I swept out of the shop and he followed along behind, just as if I was Lady Isabella—that was satisfying, too, for a moment.

The hat shop was next, but I stopped outside, pretending to look in the window.

"Jem, *why* did you believe Barlow? You trusted me not to give you away when you first asked me to take letters to Lady Isabella."

"That's different." He sounded hesitant, as if he wasn't sure he meant it.

I looked up at him, wondering if I was wasting my time trying to understand. "How is it different? Is Barlow a particular friend? I mean, was he, before he helped get you arrested?"

"No. No more than any of the other m— servants."

Menservants, he'd been going to say.

"All women, is it? Or only the likes of me?" I went into the shop without waiting for an answer, telling myself that what Jem Langton thought really didn't matter.

He didn't come inside this time, but the green of his coat visible through the window reminded me he was there. It rather spoiled the fun of having lots of someone else's money to spend, and I didn't take long over choosing a hat. My lady wouldn't want more than one.

Lady Isabella had already written to Lady Jesson asking to borrow Sarah, and I thought I'd call to arrange a time. Gloves could wait—it was really only the fabric that was needed now. I summoned Jem to take the hat box back to Marstone House.

"Where are you going?" he asked, when I turned in the opposite direction.

"I'm going to call my friend. *If* that meets with your approval." Or even if it didn't. I walked off without waiting for him to reply.

CHAPTER 18

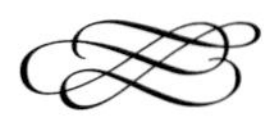

Marstone House was bustling when I returned. Lord Wingrave had already set off for Devonshire, but he'd left orders for all the bedrooms to be opened up properly—except the ones right next to Lord Marstone's suite, so as not to disturb him with noise.

Mrs Wardle was determined to make a good impression on Lady Wingrave, when she arrived for Lady Isabella's wedding. That meant a proper cleaning everywhere, including under the furniture; no matter that most things had been covered over, some dust always got in. As I was passing through the servants' hall, O'Connor staggered in. He was in his work clothes, his arms full of holland covers.

"Langton got lucky this morning, he did," he said when he saw me, and winked. "Escaping some of this. How about you take me with you next time?"

I laughed, as he'd intended. It would have felt quite different if Barlow had asked that question. I went to my room to leave my bonnet, then to see if my lady had any need of me. She was reading in the parlour, and looked up as I knocked and entered.

"Did you get some material, Molly?"

"Yes, my lady. Sarah's coming tomorrow morning to talk about styles, if that suits?"

She put the book aside. "That is convenient, thank you. I'd hoped to spend the afternoon with Mr Carterton, but he will be busy then. Although he is coming to dinner this evening." She paused for a moment, smiling to herself. "Perhaps we could see something of London? We can take the carriage, if my aunt doesn't want it. If you fetch the guidebook from the library, we can decide where we want to go."

"In the library, my lady?"

"Yes—it's in the bookcase to the left of the door."

I could find that—but picking the right book might take me some time, what with having to read all the titles on the edges.

My lady must have guessed why I was hesitating. "I'll get it, Molly, don't worry."

I didn't feel comfortable sitting down before my lady had said I could, so I looked around the parlour while I waited. A painting above the fireplace caught my eye and I went closer to examine it. It showed a large red brick house beneath a blue sky. A pretty lady sat on a fancy wooden bench with two small boys. The lady's gown was quite a bit wider in the skirts than the ones I'd seen around London, but not too different in style. Was this the last Lady Marstone, and was one of the boys Lord Wingrave?

"Slacking off, Moll?"

Barlow again! Was I never to be rid of him?

"Why did Langton get to stroll about London with you this morning, eh?" He advanced into the room as he spoke, dust marks on his clothing and face. "I get set to moving furniture at the bidding of women, and all he has to do is carry parcels. What's he got that I haven't?"

"Plenty." I was pleased my voice came out so calm. There were people within calling distance so he couldn't do much to me, but I didn't like the look in his eyes.

He was close now, and thrust his face towards mine. "I'll have you yet, Molly Simons." I backed up a step. "There won't always be other people around. Nor pots of tea to throw at me."

I backed another step, then my heel caught on something and I fell backwards, my shoulders hitting the side of the fireplace. I landed hard on the floor and the fire irons clattered beside me. Thank the Lord it was warm weather and no fire lit.

"Molly, are you all right?" Lady Isabella hurried into the room, dropping a book on a chair.

Barlow put out a hand to help me up, his face all sympathy and smiles. "She tripped, my lady. Come on Moll, clumsy girl."

I got to my feet without his help, rubbing the elbow that had struck the edge of the hearth.

"Thank you, Barlow," my lady said. "You may go."

He bowed and left. Lady Isabella waited until Barlow closed the door, then beckoned me over to the sofa. "What happened, Molly? Was he... harassing you?"

I nodded.

"Tell me."

So I did. All of it—the times at Marstone Park when I'd managed to duck out of the way, and the times when I hadn't. She'd heard about how he came to drop the parcels, but I told her about the tea as well, and what Mowbray had said afterwards—about me having to keep away from Barlow. And then Barlow's threat just now.

"Did you report those other times to Mrs Williamson, or Benning?"

"There wouldn't be any point." I told her more or less the same things I'd said to Jem that morning, but without the shouting.

"Like Sarah," she said, when I'd finished.

"Not as bad as that, my—"

"No, no. I mean about men not believing you." She stood up and rang the bell. "I think it's time we got rid of Barlow."

Mowbray himself came to answer the bell. "My lady?"

"I want a word with you about the footman, Barlow."

Mowbray looked at me, still sitting beside my lady, and his brows drew together. "Simons, I thought I told you to stay away from him?"

"*That,* Mowbray, is precisely the problem." She nodded at me. "Molly, you may leave us."

I didn't need to be told to avoid Barlow right now. I took the stairs straight up to my lady's room, and shut myself in the dressing room with some mending.

Lady Isabella came up to her room not ten minutes later, and sat in her usual chair by the window. "He'll be gone within the hour."

"Thank you, my lady."

She shook her head. "You should have told me, Molly, I could have…" Then she shrugged, the corners of her mouth turning down. We both knew that if this had happened before Lord Marstone took so ill, Benning at Marstone Park would have brushed her off. "As I had to remind Mowbray, things will be different when Will is in charge."

I wasn't sure about that. I didn't say so, but my lady saw too much sometimes.

"Will is a good man, Molly."

"I didn't mean any disrespect, my lady."

"But…? Come, Molly, you can speak freely to me."

"My lady, it depends on who he has working for him. If Mr Mowbray believes Barlow, or doesn't want to have to find a new footman, Lord Wingrave would never know about it."

She looked thoughtful. "Or Mr Carterton, I suppose. I will have to ensure the staff know what I expect of them. Why are you smiling, Molly?"

"I was just thinking I wouldn't like to be on your wrong side, my lady."

That made her chuckle. "Mr Carterton is taking me to meet his father this afternoon, Molly. My aunt thinks I should still be accompanied, so you will come with me."

"Yes, my lady. Which gown will you wear?"

"The blue, I think."

It needed a few creases pressing out, so I took it down to the laundry room. Jem stepped in while I was waiting for the irons to heat. He looked... not cross, exactly. Wary, perhaps? "Barlow's gone."

"I know."

"He was cursing you, saying it was all your fault."

This again! I turned my shoulder and picked up one of the irons to test it.

"Moll, you don't understand. *I'm* not saying it's your fault."

"Oh? That makes a change." I regretted snapping at him as soon as I said it.

"I thought about what you said this morning. I'm sorry."

"Hmm." He did look sincere. Although I was pleased that he'd apologised, it wasn't enough—not if he was going to carry on judging women without knowing the facts.

"Thing is, Moll, Barlow was threatening to pay you back for it. I think he meant it. You'd best not go out alone—not for a while."

I put the iron down—my lady's gowns were too fine to risk me scorching them because I wasn't concentrating. "Thank you for warning me." I'd have to tell my lady, but O'Connor could go with me if she sent me on any errands. Or Jem, if he'd really meant that apology.

"I told Sprout to keep his eyes open," he added, "in case Barlow loiters around here."

"Thank you." The idea that Jem had done it to keep me safe was warming. "That lad must be earning a lot of pennies."

"More than you think." He smiled. "Lord Wingrave is paying him a couple of shillings a week to be inconspicuous and keep an eye on things."

That seemed odd, but then many of the things the quality did seemed strange to me. I suppose he might be worried about Fancy Man or his Spanish friends.

"Langton, get your arse up to the dining room!" O'Connor stuck his head through the door. "Stop dallying with your woman now and come and help move the table." He winked, and went off.

I felt my face get hot at the idea of being Jem's woman—something I'd wanted until a couple of weeks ago. And now wanted again.

Interestingly, I thought the back of Jem's neck had turned a little pink as he followed O'Connor.

Lady Isabella had decided on Westminster Abbey for our excursion the following afternoon, and ordered the carriage. I didn't think Barlow would do anything when I was with my lady, so I didn't tell her what Jem had said. But I did catch Sprout's eye as we left the house, and he came trotting up.

"Barlow?"

He shook his head. "Not seen 'im, miss."

That was all right then. I nodded and he wandered off again. I reckoned that if Barlow *was* going to try anything, he'd be following me from Marstone House, not hoping to run across me somewhere else in London.

The Abbey was very fine inside—finer even than Marstone Park. I got a stiff neck peering up at the ceiling—all the little stone beams fanning out from the pillars looked too delicate to be holding the roof up. We wandered around for a little while, then my lady paid sixpence each for us to look at the waxwork figures and the tombs. That was much more interesting. I hadn't heard of most of the dead kings and queens—only King Charles, because his face was on the inn sign in Over Minster, hiding in an oak tree. But I enjoyed looking at the different clothes they had on. I didn't reckon much to some of the lying down carvings, though. Their clothes looked just like a normal standing up statue had been laid on its back. The best thing was a skeleton dressed in a hood and gown—it looked more real than the carvings on the tombs and gave me the shivers.

It sounds ungrateful to say so, but I enjoyed the next afternoon more. Lady Isabella was to go to Lady Jesson's, and didn't need me. When I explained about Barlow's threat, she rang for Mowbray and told him that Langton was to escort me wherever I wanted to go.

"Langton knows Barlow best, I think," my lady said when Mowbray had gone. "And O'Connor doesn't look quite as capable of protecting you." She had a little smile, as if those weren't the only reasons she'd picked Jem.

Half an hour later we climbed the area steps together. Jem had left off his livery and wig, which I was pleased about. It was one thing to have a footman in all his finery following me around when I was on an errand for my lady. It wouldn't have felt right this afternoon.

"Where d'you want to go, Molly?"

"You tell me. You come from London."

He thought for a moment. "The Tower of London. That's where King Henry beheaded two of his wives. There are wild animals to see, as well."

"Ooh, yes. Is it far?"

"Three or four miles—we'll get a hackney."

"I didn't bring much money..." It wasn't fair that he should pay because my lady had asked him to escort me, although if Lord Wingrave had been as generous to him as to me, Jem must have a fair bit of coin right now.

"I'll pay, Moll." He sounded offended. Almost as if he'd asked me to walk out with him this afternoon.

"Why did King Henry have two wives?" I asked as we set off towards Bond Street. "And why did he chop their heads off?"

"He had six wives." He waved, and a hackney pulled up beside us. Jem told the driver where we wanted to go, and climbed in beside me.

Six wives? I waited for him to mock my ignorance, but he didn't.

"Divorced the first one, beheaded the second. The third one died having a baby." He was counting them off on his fingers. "Divorced the fourth, beheaded the fifth, and he died before the sixth one got on his wrong side."

"Lucky lady. Did you go to school, then, to know all that?"

His mouth turned down for a moment, as if I'd said something wrong, but then he answered in quite a normal voice. "For a while, and I've tried to improve myself."

The journey was much nicer than when we went to St Giles. For one thing, the carriage was clean. Jem pointed out different buildings as we passed—the best one was St Paul's Cathedral, towering white above the houses around it.

"They used to take traitors into the Tower by boat," he told me, when there were only houses to see outside. "Queen Elizabeth was sent there when she was only a girl."

"Can we see the river, too? I've never seen so much water at once."

He laughed at me, but in a kind way. "We can do whatever you like, Moll. Look, we're here now."

The Tower didn't appear too grim in the sunshine, but it must have looked quite different if you were to be imprisoned there. Jem had lots to say when he'd paid for us to go in, telling me about the ravens, and some of the famous traitors executed on the green. I forgot most of it almost as soon as he said it, but he had a nice, deep voice and I was enjoying just walking with him.

I hoped he *did* think of it as walking out together.

CHAPTER 19

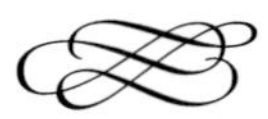

Lord Marstone lingered on. Lady Isabella wasn't confined to the house, but Lady Cerney said it wouldn't be right for the two of them to attend balls and other engagements, so I had much less to do. My lady still went for drives with Mr Carterton or Lady Jesson, but her ball gowns stayed unused in the dressing room and I had no occasion to practise the fancy hairstyles needed. Tamworth had said she didn't have any more to teach me, so I had a lot more free time than I was used to.

Lady Isabella caught me in the dressing room with a book one day—not that she minded me reading, for I'd completed all my duties. But when I explained, she helped me find some suitable books in the library, and assisted me when I got stuck on some of the words. And she gave me paper to practise my writing.

The week after we went to the Tower, my lady arranged for Jem and me to have the afternoon off at the same time. Jem looked to be as pleased about it as I was, which made me even happier.

We took a hackney again, and it seemed to me that we went the same way as last time—but we got out before the Tower, at the bottom of a tall pillar. A really tall pillar, quite wide, and with a door at the bottom.

"What's this, then?"

"It's a monument to the fire." He smiled at me. "I'll tell you about it at the top. Ready?"

"Of course."

He paid our sixpences and we went in, Jem looking over his shoulder now and then to make sure I was keeping up as we climbed the steps. I did, but I was quite out of breath when we reached the top and went through the door.

"Oh!" I should have expected the view, I suppose, but I was still surprised to see London spread out before me, the people below looking like tiny dolls. There was a breeze up here that I hadn't felt at ground level, but the sun kept me warm enough.

"A lot of London burned down a hundred years ago," Jem said. "That's why the buildings around here are fairly new." He pointed towards St Paul's, its dome sticking up above the rooftops, then gave me his arm and we walked slowly around the platform. On the other side, the tops of the Tower of London looked quite close, and ships' masts showed beyond the houses.

"Why are there so many ships here and not further up the river?" I hadn't seen any masts that tall when I went to the river with Sprout.

"They can't get any further up the river because of the bridge. London Bridge, just down there." He pointed, and I felt stupid. I should have been able to work that out for myself. "There are warehouses along the shore there, on both sides of the river. Some unload their cargoes into barges to go upriver."

"Did you learn that from books as well?"

He didn't answer straight away. "No," he said at last. I expected him to say where he *had* learned it—most people would—but he didn't. I looked out over London again, but now the silence felt a little awkward.

"Have you seen enough?" he finally asked. "I thought you might like to go back by boat—you said last time that you wanted to see the river."

Those small boats I'd watched with Sprout? I wasn't too keen on the idea, but Jem had tried to please me and it wouldn't do to spoil the day. "That will be lovely, thank you."

It wasn't far to the river. I almost changed my mind when I saw the boats waiting there, the watermen resting on their oars. The boats weren't very big, and rocked whenever anyone in them moved.

"They're perfectly safe." Jem descended a few steps and held one hand out. I swallowed hard and allowed him to help me in, sitting down hastily as the thing moved beneath my feet.

"Don't worry, love." One of the watermen winked at me. "We 'aven't drowned no-one in at least a month."

"That is very reassuring, sir." I managed a smile, which turned into a genuine one a few minutes after we set off. It didn't feel nearly as bad as I'd thought. The ships beyond the bridge looked much bigger now I was sitting down at water level. "Where have they all come from?"

"All over the world," Jem said. He didn't seem inclined to say more, so I sat back and looked around. Here were some of the barges Jem had mentioned; the shouts of men unloading them carried across the water, as did smells—fish, sawdust from the timber yards, the yeasty scent of beer brewing, along with a general stink that must be coming from the mud beginning to show either side of the water.

We passed under another bridge, and now there were some huge stone buildings to our right, in between the wharves, and gardens running down to the water's edge. When the men finally pulled in to another stair, I recognised the bridge where Sprout and I had eaten pies together.

"That was lovely, Jem. Thank you."

"My pleasure." He put his arm around my shoulders and gave me a quick hug. "Shall we get something to eat? There are a couple of good places I know. Or we could buy something and eat it in the park."

"The park," I decided. The sky was still blue, the sun still warm—and I didn't want to share Jem with other folks in an alehouse or tavern.

"The park it is, then." It wasn't the same park that I'd been in with Lady Isabella, but it had grass enough to sit on. We found a woman selling meat pies and bought paper cones full of cherries from another, and Jem spread his coat on the ground for me.

"Why did you become a footman?" I asked, once we'd finished the pies. "There must be all sorts of trades you could have been apprenticed to in London." Unlike me—there wasn't much I could have done to earn a living besides going into service, not in a tiny village like Over Minster.

"It costs money to get an apprenticeship, and then you're bound for seven years usually. If you have a bad master, there's nothing you can do about it. Someone suggested that a fine looking man like me would easily get a footman's job." He seemed embarrassed to say it, although it was no more than the truth. "They were right, and the skills weren't difficult to learn. I had a couple of positions, then the man at the registry sent me to Marstone House with Barlow when they wanted footmen, and they took us on as a pair. That was four years ago."

He glanced at me sideways. "Barlow was a bit lazy, but we had a good laugh. He used to talk about... about the maids sometimes, but I thought it was just talk, or that they really did like him."

Barlow was good at pretending, but most servants were.

"My father was a clerk in one of the customs houses." Jem was looking into the distance. "My mother was pretty—really pretty. Men liked her, and she liked them too much."

That didn't sound good. I didn't speak, though.

"She ran off once, when I was six, and my father took to the bottle. She came back a few months later, saying how sorry she was and she'd made a mistake. But the talk was that her lover had thrown her out. I didn't understand at the time, but I remembered what people had said, and worked it out later. She stayed at home for a while, looking after me. Then she started to see other men again, and Dad drank even more. When he lost his job because of the drink he tried to make a living on the docks—he was tall, like me. But he couldn't make enough to keep her happy and she went off again, and never came back. He fell in the river one day."

I could see from his face that his dad had drowned. With a mother like that, it wasn't surprising he didn't think much of women. That didn't explain why he thought that most women were out to trap men into marriage, though—had his mother done that with his father? It crossed my mind that his father might not actually be his father, but that was no business of mine and made no difference to me anyway.

"How did you manage after that?" It could not have been easy for a young boy suddenly orphaned.

He shrugged. "The supervisor at the customs office was a good man—he paid me a little for sweeping up and running errands, and let me sleep in a storeroom. I scrounged meals here and there until I was big enough to work in a warehouse. That was a couple of years before I got my first job as a footman."

I suppose that explained why he was ambitious, too—wanting a good job so he'd never have to scrounge again. My family never had money to spare, but we'd never really gone short, either.

Jem got to his feet, and put out a hand to pull me up. "That's enough maudlin sentiment for one day, Moll. Sorry to—"

"Don't be daft, Jem. You wanted to explain, and you have. Not all women are like your ma."

He hadn't actually said sorry for thinking the worst of Sarah, or making similar assumptions about me, but I reckon that story was as good as an apology. It had rather dampened our mood, though, and we walked back arm in arm through the parks in silence. A friendly silence.

We returned to find nearly everyone sitting around the table in the servants' hall, drinking ale and tea. Even Mowbray and Mrs Wardle were sitting there, alongside the scullery maids.

"His Lordship is dead," Mowbray announced. "Not half an hour ago." His words sounded a little slurred, and I wondered if he'd been at the port again.

I couldn't see any signs of grief in the faces around the table, just the same air of waiting that most of us had felt ever since Lord Wingrave stopped Lady Isabella's sham marriage. I suppose it was natural, really—we all knew what the old lord was like, and stayed out of his way as much as we could. No-one knew how Lord Wingrave would be as a master, or even if he'd want to keep everyone on.

"We'll have a proper mistress again," Mrs Wardle said. "I remember the last Lady Marstone—a lovely lady, she was."

"We might have parties and balls again!" Sally suggested, a gleam of excitement in her eye.

"More work…" Cook looked tired.

I left them to their speculation, and went to tidy my hair before seeing if Lady Isabella needed anything. She was sitting at her little table writing a letter, but put her pen down when I entered.

"It's strange, Molly," she said, looking out at the darkening sky. "He was alive this morning, and now he's not—but I don't feel any different. He didn't ask to see me."

"He was probably too ill, my lady."

She nodded, but I guessed she thought the same as me—her father wasn't like to have asked for her unless it was to make her do his bidding, and that time had passed.

"I'm writing to Will—he'll come straight away, I think."

Poor Lord Wingrave; he couldn't have been back home for more than a week. "Shouldn't Mr Staverton be dealing with things, my lady? Or Lady Cerney?"

"My aunt's gone to a card party, but I don't know where. Mowbray will send to Marstone Park for Staverton to come."

"I'm not sure…" I didn't like telling tales, but my lady was already displeased with Mowbray for the way he'd ignored Barlow's behaviour. "That is, I think he won't get around to that until tomorrow, my lady."

"In his cups, is he?"

I didn't think she'd notice something like that. "Er, not quite that bad, my lady." Not yet.

"Don't worry, Molly, I already knew he's been emptying the cellar. He smelled of drink when I was talking to him about Barlow."

Silly old fool, thinking he'd get away with drinking on duty because there were only ladies in the house.

"I'll write to Staverton as well. Send someone to fetch Archer, will you? He can take my letter to Devonshire. And find someone to ride to Marstone Park."

"Yes, my lady." I don't know if it was her father having died, or her betrothal to Mr Carterton, but Lady Isabella seemed to have turned from a girl into a proper lady, ready to take charge of things when she had to.

The house was at sixes and sevens for the next week. Lord Wingrave —now Lord Marstone—arrived four days later. My lady and Lady Cerney had gone into blacks, and received condolence calls in the parlour. His new lordship interviewed Mrs Wardle and Mowbray; Mowbray emerged from his interview looking rather pale.

And Sprout told me that he'd seen Barlow hanging around in the square.

He told Jem, too, and Jem must have told his lordship, for I was summoned to the library. I found Jem already sitting there, facing his lordship across the desk, and an empty chair ready for me beside him.

"Lady Isabella told me about your trouble with Barlow," his lordship started.

I was pleased I didn't have to describe it all again.

"You cannot have his threat hanging over you—he sounds like the kind of man who will bear a grudge for a long time." His eyes shifted for a moment to the portrait of his father above the fireplace.

"Yes, my lord."

"We have come up with a plan, but it requires some courage from you, Molly. If you don't wish to do it, we will think of something else."

We? I glanced at Jem, who seemed to be sitting a little taller. His lordship was an unusual man, consulting a footman.

"Merely warning him off will be insufficient, I think," his lordship went on, "even if I do so myself. I could have him arrested on some trumped up charge, but I do not wish to descend to his level. No, he needs to be caught actually doing something for which he can be transported."

That didn't sound good to me. "What would I have to do, my lord?"

"Bait a trap."

He seemed to be waiting for me to say something. I swallowed hard, but nodded.

"Very well. You will go out with an escort two or three times. Langton, or O'Connor."

Buying gloves or undergarments would be a good enough excuse.

"Then you will do the same thing, but with no escort. No *visible* escort, I should say. I will arrange for you to be watched at every point along your journey, and also followed at a discreet distance. We are hoping to catch Barlow in the act."

I looked at Jem.

"We'll keep you safe, Moll," he promised. I believed him, but it still sounded dangerous to me.

CHAPTER 20

We started the plan the next day, when Sprout reported that Barlow was in the square again. I walked to Bond Street with Jem. He was the proper footman, in wig and livery, walking beside me but obviously not walking out with me—merely two servants doing their mistress' bidding. We didn't go the way I knew, but a different route that took us through narrower streets, and past lots of entrances to mews and small alleys.

Good places to be attacked.

I felt nervous, even though Jem was with me, and it spoiled the fun of buying ribbons and trims. We did the same thing two days later. And again, two days after that.

The third time, Jem set out with me as usual then pretended to forget something and returned to the house. I walked on through the same narrow streets as before, somewhat reassured by seeing Sprout loitering on a corner ahead. He gave no sign that he knew me, and I did my best to ignore him as I passed. My knees felt wobbly, and I was really, really wishing I'd said no to his lordship's suggestion.

Nothing happened—I got to Bond Street, and walked on to the far end. If Barlow was watching, it would look suspicious if I came home empty-handed, so I bought a length of lace. After that, it was really tempting to keep to the wider streets, but if I didn't give Barlow a chance to show his hand I'd have to do all this again.

I set off back the way I'd come, my stomach knotted so hard I felt sick. Twice I turned around when I heard footsteps behind me, and twice the person walked on past and took no notice at all. Perhaps Barlow hadn't seen me come—

"Got you, bitch!"

I barely heard the words as I was dragged sideways into the entrance to a mews, Barlow's hand clasped tight around one arm. I was too shocked to even scream for help. He moved fast, and I tripped over my skirts, only his grip on my arm stopping a complete fall.

"Get up!" he hissed, but I stumbled and fell again as he dragged me, my breath coming in sharp pants. He pushed open a door, and then I was in a stable, shoved onto a pile of straw.

"No character, no job. *Your* fault."

I scrabbled backwards, trying to stand at the same time as getting away from him. But he'd thrown me into an empty stall, and I had nowhere to go.

"Help! He—"

His unwashed stink filled my nostrils as he clamped one hand across my mouth. "Shut up, bitch. There's no-one here." His weight held me down as he started to pull up my skirt with his other hand.

"Wrong!"

Barlow's weight was suddenly gone. Behind him, silhouetted against the light from the door, two men stepped back and away, leaving a third holding one of Barlow's arms twisted up behind his back. Jem. He'd said I could trust him.

Then Jem let Barlow go.

I scrambled further into the stall, afraid that I'd not been saved at all, but Jem came in after and crouched down. "Don't worry, Moll, you're safe now."

"Oh, Jem!" And I burst into tears. He put his arm around my shoulders, and I turned into him, burying my head in his shoulder.

"Sorry, love. He was a little faster than we'd anticipated. Did he hurt you?"

"Not really." A couple of bruises where I'd fallen, probably, and some on my arm, too.

He eased me away from him, peering into my face in the dim light. "Did he hurt you, Molly?" he asked again. His tone was more urgent, and I realised my first answer had been muffled by his coat. "I'll kill the—"

"I'm not hurt, Jem, just bruised." I sniffed, and fumbled for a handkerchief to blow my nose. "But you let him go!"

He pulled me to my feet and led me towards the door. "Not exactly. I let him think he could escape." His arm came around me while I took in what was happening in the cobbled mews. Barlow was fighting against someone I didn't recognise, onlookers being kept back by a man blocking the alley in each direction. One of them was Mr Archer. I was in no further danger, that was clear, but it was Jem's arm around me that gave me that feeling, not the presence of the others.

Then, as a blow to the face finally felled Barlow, I *did* recognise his opponent. The new Lord Marstone, but dressed in clothes that were fit only for a labourer. He touched his own face as he regarded Barlow sprawled on the ground, and there were red marks where Barlow must have hit him. He was breathing hard, but his smile showed satisfaction.

"Get up," my lord said, and nodded at Mr Archer when Barlow didn't move. Then Barlow had one arm up behind his back again, Mr Archer forcing him to stand.

"What d'you do that for?" Barlow whined. "She's only a servant girl."

"Oh, I agree that a magistrate may not be too concerned about a maidservant," his lordship said. "But attacking a peer of the realm? That will have you in gaol at the very least."

"That's why I let him go," Jem said quietly, as Barlow's jaw dropped. Then Barlow started to plead that he hadn't known, and how was he expected to tell when his lordship was dressed like that?

"It was his lordship's idea," Jem said.

"He fought for me?" A lord fighting for a servant?

Jem laughed. "Not entirely—he thought it was a way of getting rid of Barlow without having to go to court. He wasn't risking much, really, with us around in case he lost. But like you told me before, Barlow could have said you'd invited him, and only changed your mind later. There'd only be your word against his. "

"But if my lord doesn't want...?"

"Shhh." Jem jerked his head towards his lordship. Barlow had finally stopped whining.

"I could have you up before a magistrate," my lord said, almost as if he was having a conversation. "Or perhaps have my men drop you in the river."

"Please, my lord, I didn't—"

"Or you might offer your services to the Navy."

"His lordship can arrange for him to be on a ship bound for the East Indies," Jem explained, as two of Mr Archer's men led Barlow away. "With a captain who knows what he's done."

"The Navy may not thank me for it," his lordship commented, coming over to where we stood. "Are you all right, Molly? It was very brave of you, allowing yourself to be put in harm's way."

"Thank you, my lord." It felt good, knowing that Barlow would not be around to get his revenge. "If I hadn't, the same thing might have happened without anyone to help me."

"Just so." He smiled. "Now, I'd better get back before anyone recognises me in this clothing." He looked down at his tattered trousers in distaste. "Langton, take her for a stiff drink, or whatever she wants." He nodded at us, and followed the last of his men out of the mews.

I wasn't sure about a drink—my legs still felt shaky. "Can we just walk, Jem? In the park?"

"Let's go to Green Park, and get some milk from the cows there. We can go for an ale afterwards, if you feel better by then."

I took his arm, and we had the milk, but not the ale. Although I knew I was safe now, I had an urge to curl up in a corner and cry. I asked Jem to take me back to Marstone House, and he did, his presence beside me comforting.

"Jem?"

"Hmm?"

"You won't tell anyone else, will you? I don't... I mean, there'd be questions, and—"

"Course I won't." He turned to face me. "Trust his lordship to get rid of Barlow, Molly."

I nodded.

"I shouldn't have agreed to the plan. I'm sorry, Molly, that we didn't—"

"I agreed, too." I blinked, not wanting to cry in front of him. "At least he'll be gone now, and won't bother anyone again. I'm sure that in a day or two, I'll think it was worth it."

"That's my girl." And he hugged my shoulders before we went indoors.

His lordship must have said something to Lady Isabella, for she asked me if I was well, and said I could retire early if I wished.

"No, thank you, my lady." My legs had stopped feeling shaky by now, and I thought if I went to bed before I was sleepy, I was more like to remember being dragged into that stable and give myself nightmares.

"My wedding will be in three weeks, Molly." She walked into the dressing room as she spoke. "Here, in the house, as we are in mourning."

"You'll not wear black for your wedding, my lady?" Black didn't become her—it made her skin look pasty.

"No. I thought I would ask Fletcher to make me a new gown for the occasion. What colour do you think?"

I didn't know if she really wanted to discuss it, or if she was trying to take my mind off what had just happened, but it did the trick. We settled on something in the combination of cream and gold that suited her so well, and Sarah was to help decide on the design. "Something suitable for a married woman," my lady said, with a twinkle in her eye.

"As long as you don't have a neckline as low as that woman we saw in the park." I said it beneath my breath, but she heard, and laughed.

Lady Isabella kept busy over the next couple of weeks, even though she couldn't go to the usual parties and theatres and the like. I went with her when Mr Carterton took us, with Sarah, to look for premises for her new business. Sarah protested when she first heard the idea, saying that Lady Isabella had already helped her a lot, but Mr Carterton explained about contracts and loans, and that it was really an investment they were making. She went right off to see if Dawkins and a couple of the others from Madame Donnard's would work for her, and my lady and Lady Jesson both put orders in for lots of gowns before the place had even been redecorated. Sarah looked happy, really happy, and it brought a lump to my throat that Lady Isabella had thought of all this even while she was worried about her own future.

My lady still gave me plenty of extra time off. Jem took me to see the Horse Guards parading one morning, and very stirring it was, with music playing and all the fine uniforms and horses. Others watching had children with them, laughing in delight at the spectacle. With Jem standing tall beside me, I couldn't help imagining a boy on his shoulders with his father's brown eyes. Or with my grey ones.

There were lots more horses at Astley's Amphitheatre, too, when we went one evening. Telling me about his father had changed Jem—he was more open, and he talked to me about the happy times when he was young, for there had been some. He even heard all about my family without looking bored.

It was a fine evening when we came out of Astley's, with the sky beginning to fade to a darker blue. We walked back across the bridge together arm in arm, and the warm feeling of being close to him was lovely. Jem stopped beneath a tree in Green Park, his face only a pale glimmer in the dusk.

"Fancy a kiss, Moll?"

For an instant, I heard Barlow's voice in my head. But Barlow had demanded, not asked, and Jem was leaning against the tree, making no move towards me. If you were watching from a distance, you might think he wasn't really interested at all, but there had been something in his voice that told me he wanted it.

I took a step towards him, then his words from the past came into my mind—the words about women entrapping men, of getting with child to make a man marry them. I stopped, still an arm's length way.

"Just a kiss, Molly."

He'd changed, these last few weeks. And I wanted to stand closer, to find out what a proper kiss was like.

"It's been grand, walking out with you," he went on. "I'll miss you when you go off with Lady Isabella."

Oh.

I felt like someone had thrown cold water over me.

He'd never suggested there might be more than walking out together but, silly me, I'd thought this had the possibility of leading somewhere. *Hoped* it might. I hadn't thought what, though. One of us would have to give up our position, and with Jem's ambition it wasn't going to be him.

"Best not." My voice came out a lot more evenly than I'd expected. "I might like it too much."

"That's the strangest excuse..." He leaned closer, peering at my face. "Moll, are you all right? Did I say something wrong?"

If he was to be fixed in London or at Marstone Park, and I was to be with Lady Isabella, it was right that he'd made that clear now.

"No. But like you said, we'll be in different places soon."

"I wish it wasn't so. But I've got... I mean, Lord Marstone... He's going to have Mowbray train me as under-butler. I'll not get a chance as good as that anywhere else."

"It's all right, Jem. I won't get as good a chance again as I've had with Lady Isabella. I'd be foolish to give that up." Particularly for someone who'd only wanted a kiss.

Lady Marstone would have no use for me—she must already have her own maid. So if I stayed, I'd be going back to emptying chamber pots and the like, even if his lordship allowed his staff to marry. And Jem hadn't said anything to make me think he wanted that; it was my own wishes that had made me imagine something more.

At least I'd have some nice memories. "I've enjoyed our outings, too, Jem. But I think we should stop now."

There was silence for a moment, then he sighed. "We'd best get back, then." He offered his arm, and I took it.

My lady's sisters arrived with their husbands, and with the house filling up I didn't have much time to miss Jem. Apart from at night, alone in my little attic room. I couldn't help wondering then what it would be like to lie with him, and to have him to talk to every day.

I'd last seen Lady Isabella's sisters a year ago, before they were taken to London for their season—and had *not* married men the old lord had chosen for them. They both looked happy and content with their husbands, and Lady Elizabeth had a lovely little boy, a couple of months old. Betsy, who'd been maid to both the young ladies, was now Lady Elizabeth's woman; we had a good gossip about the people at Marstone Park during the last year, and she told me all about Lady Elizabeth's new home in Yorkshire. Lady Theresa had married a mere 'mister'—which must have angered his old lordship no end. He was a more intense man, with dark hair and eyes, but you could tell he doted on his wife, and she on him, from the way they looked at each other.

The new Lady Marstone was lovely, too. She was big with child, so she spent most of her days in the parlour that looked out over the garden. Lord Wingrave spent as much time with her and their two little girls as he could, but he was often busy with some kind of government business during the day. The girls could behave when they had to, but the older one spent a lot of time—and energy—running around in the garden, with the younger trying to copy her.

I tried to stop myself thinking about having children of my own. There'd be someone else, I told myself. Ma hadn't married until she was twenty-five, so there was time yet, and I'd be meeting more people when I went to the Carterton's country estate with my lady.

Does trying to cheer yourself up like that ever work?

My lady was married in the back parlour, and only the family were there with the priest—a proper one, this time. As soon as all the dishes for the wedding feast were laid out in the dining room, all us servants had our own celebration in the servants' hall, with food quite as fine as above stairs. I didn't stay until all the food was gone, as Mr and the new Mrs Carterton were to set off for Sussex early in the afternoon, and I was to go ahead with Mr Carterton's valet and the luggage. I didn't feel much like celebrating either. I wouldn't see Jem again for a long time, not if my lady chose to spend most of her time in Sussex.

It was probably for the best. That's what I told myself.

Jem joined me as I waited near the front steps for the carriage to arrive. He'd left off his wig and fancy coat, and looked all the better for it. This was the Jem I'd come to like too much for my own good, not the stiff, formal one in his uniform. "Take care, Molly. I *will* miss you."

"And I, you."

I was beginning to regret not having that kiss—it would have been something to remember—but it was too late now.

CHAPTER 21

Oakley Place was nowhere near the size of Marstone Park, nor did it have such fancy marble floors and silk wall coverings. I liked it better, though, apart from being half a day's travel on the other side of London. I wouldn't be able to go and see Ma on my afternoons off.

The house had a large lawn in front, and a low hill behind covered in trees. It felt lighter and more cheerful than the Park, but that was more to do with the people in it than the place itself. Everyone was friendly, and I soon settled in.

My lady and her husband went for walks in the woods and drives in an open carriage. When they changed for dinner in the evening my lady chose to wear only her simple gowns, so although I spent some time cleaning muddy hems on her walking dresses, I didn't have fancy silks and satins to take care of.

The housekeeper there was about the same age as Mrs Wardle, and just as efficient. But she was thinner and smiled at people more. Andrews, the butler, was much younger than Mowbray, and so was Mr Carterton's valet. I still missed the gossip of the servants' hall, but dining with those three was much more enjoyable than sharing Mrs Wardle's room with Mowbray and Tamworth in London. All three of them often spent their spare time with a book, and happily discussed what they'd read over dinner or our evening supper.

The valet escorted me on a tour of the grounds one day. He was a pleasant man, and if it hadn't been for Jem I think we might even have walked out together. I couldn't help noticing the lack of the warmer feelings that I'd experienced with Jem, though.

I did miss him. I even went so far as to think about asking Fletcher to employ me as a seamstress so I could move back to London, but it would have been folly to give up my position with Lady Isabella for the sake of a man who'd said nothing more than that he would miss me. It wasn't enough for a good life together, and that was what I wanted.

After about a month, things had cooled a little between my lady and her husband—by which I mean they managed to be apart for several hours at a time before going in search of the other. It was a bit of a relief, to be honest. It was hard seeing the way they looked at each other, when I was still thinking of the man I wanted to have looking at me like that.

My lady surprised me one evening. She was in one of the filmy, lacy robes Lady Jesson had given her as a wedding gift, and I was brushing her hair.

"Carterton has business in Town, Molly, so we are removing there the day after tomorrow."

"Back to London, my lady?" Would I see Jem? I wanted to, but I wasn't sure if that would be wise.

I'd have to think about that later; Lady Isabella was still talking. "Ma'am, if you please. You know I don't bother with my title." She shook her head, despite me still having my brush in it.

"It's hard to get out of the habit of years, my... ma'am. Besides, you'll be Lady Carterton some day."

"That day is a long way off, I hope. But that's another reason to go back. Lord Carterton was unwell earlier in the year, and Carterton doesn't want to leave him alone there for too long."

"There, ma'am." I put the brush down, leaving her hair down around her shoulders.

She met my eyes in the mirror. "Will you be pleased to be back in London, Molly? There must be some sights you haven't seen yet."

"Yes, ma'am. The countryside's a bit quiet for my tastes." That was the truth—it was pretty, but there was nothing in particular I wanted to do when I had my first full afternoon off. That never used to bother me when I was at Marstone Park—I'd happily walk the same path to Over Minster and back again. The places and people to see in London had spoiled me for country living.

Perhaps in London I could walk out with Jem again. It would be easy enough, as the house in Brook Street wasn't far from Grosvenor Square. I'd have to think hard about seeing Jem again, though, for we would end up having another parting when my lady moved back to Sussex.

My lady's room looked out over the front of the house. Late the next afternoon I was finishing packing her trunk ready for the journey to London when I noticed a rider coming up the drive. Not much of a rider—he looked more like a sack of coal perched on the saddle. His hat shaded his face, and when he came closer to the house I couldn't see him without leaning out of the window, so I went back to my packing.

It wasn't until I went down to the servants' hall that I realised why the rider had looked so bad on a horse. There, sitting next to one of the footmen, was Jem—large as life, and with a mug of ale in front of him.

I must have stood in the doorway for a full ten seconds, astounded to see him there. Delight gave way to wondering if he was only here with a message for my lady or Mr Carterton. But surely a groom would have been sent if it was only a matter of a message?

"Jem." It wasn't much more than a whisper, but he heard me and looked up.

"Hello, Molly." He smiled, rather uncertainly, and stood up. "It's nice out—come for a walk with me?"

Had he brought bad news? Ma? Word might have been sent to Marstone House if something had happened.

No—he wouldn't be smiling at me in that case. "All right. But… I mean, I should check with my lady."

The footman spoke up. "Mistress said you could go." He winked at Jem and returned to his book.

There was only one way to find out why he was here. The back entrance to the house led out to the stable yard and the kitchen garden, and I stopped on the path beside the peas—we were out of sight here from the gardeners weeding the salad beds.

Jem looked at his feet, then at the peas. Then he cleared his throat, but still didn't say anything.

"I didn't know you could ride," I said, when the silence became uncomfortable. He grimaced, and I couldn't help smiling. He must have been in the saddle most of the day. "Sore muscles? I didn't know riding was part of an under-butler's duties."

"Not normally, no. Lord Marstone—the new one, I mean…"

I nodded. I still associated that title with the old tyrant and had to think twice when someone said it.

"Lord Marstone is… unusual. He wants his staff to be able to do more than just their job."

"You're to be a groom as well as under-butler?" I widened my eyes, and he chuckled.

"Don't be daft, Moll. He said he never knew when he'd need to send a trusted man with a message."

And Jem was a trusted man—that much had already been clear. "You've only just started learning, then. I saw you arrive."

His grin was rueful. "Was it that obvious?"

"I'm afraid so. It must have been urgent for his lordship to send so poor a rider." Not that I believed that. I didn't know, but Jem's wary look, the oddness of his arrival, were beginning to make me hope that he'd come to see *me*. "Besides, we're all going to London tomorrow. I thought my lady would have told Lord Marstone. Why send you here today?"

"Tomorrow? I didn't know that." His face turned a little red. "His lordship didn't exactly send me. I… er…" He cleared his throat and started again. "Lord Marstone said he had a position in mind for you at Marstone House, if you were interested, and I could let you know next time I saw you. I couldn't wait, Moll. Mowbray didn't mind me taking a couple of days away, and I borrowed a horse."

He wouldn't have come all this way only to tell me about a position, would he? I knew what I wanted him to be here for, but I might be getting my hopes up for nothing. Again.

"I always did think you were a pretty one, Molly."

I felt myself blushing now. "You never showed it." Not until he asked for that kiss.

"Yes, well…" He looked away, his mouth turned down.

"Your ma?"

He nodded.

"That's past, Jem. Not all women are like her."

"I know. I mean, I knew that anyway, with my head, but it wasn't easy to believe it with my heart. But you, and Lady Isabella—neither of you would behave like she did."

"No, we wouldn't."

"I missed you, Molly. I knew I would before you left, but I didn't know how much."

This could not be about a job—Jem wouldn't be looking nervous if all he was doing was passing on a message from Lord Marstone. "I couldn't stop thinking about you, either." Maybe I'd agree to a kiss this time, after all. "Jem—why did he decide to offer me a job in London?"

"I asked him to."

"Why?"

"Molly, will you marry me? We'd be able to..."

Marry?

Oh, yes, I wanted to. But it seemed very sudden on his part, going from asking for a kiss to wanting to marry me. Rushing into things was what got a lot of people into trouble.

"Are you sure about this, Jem?"

"Sure as I've ever been about anything, Molly. What do you say?" He smiled his lovely smile at me.

Yes.

I needed to get a few things clear between us before I gave him my answer, though. I folded my arms, and his smile vanished.

"What is this position then? Chambermaid?" It might well be worth going back to emptying slops to be with Jem.

"No, no. Much better than that—housekeeper."

Housekeeper? Me? But my doubts about that could wait.

"What do you say, Moll?"

"*If* I say yes, Jem Langton, there will be conditions."

His mouth dropped open for a moment. "What… what conditions?"

"If anyone says anything bad about me, you do not believe them."

"Of course I w—"

"And if anyone does the same about my friends, you find out what the other side of the story is before making any judgement."

"Yes, but—"

"And even if it seems obvious that they must have done something wrong—like having a bastard child—you consider that they may have had no choice in the matter."

He just nodded this time.

"And when you're Lord Marstone's butler and in charge of the footmen, you don't believe what they say just because they're men. You don't allow them to bother the maids."

He ran a hand through his hair, leaving bits of it sticking up. It made him look like a small boy who'd just received a scolding, and I had to stop myself from smoothing it down.

"Molly, I'm sorry for the things I said. Truly. Sometimes… Well, I've been thinking that way for ten years or more, and sometimes it's difficult to change. But I will try." One corner of his mouth curled up. "I'm sure you'll tell me if I go wrong."

"That I will!"

"Lord Marstone said we can live in the house until—"

"Jem—stop talking and kiss me."

He did, and it was as lovely as I'd hoped. The warmth of the sunshine was nothing to the feeling that spread through me as his arms held me close and our lips met. It was only when one of the gardeners cleared his throat—loudly—that we broke apart.

I felt my face go hot, but the gardener just rolled his eyes as he pushed his wheelbarrow past, and muttered something about walking in the woods.

"This way." I took Jem's hand and led him on, through the gate in the back wall of the garden. The cool shade beneath the trees was welcome, and there would be no-one to disturb us here. I could understand why some girls got led astray.

Jem found a fallen tree for us to sit on, and put his arm around me. "We can have a room at Marstone House," he explained. "Until any babes come."

I blushed at the thought of what we'd do to get those babes. The idea of it suddenly didn't seem strange any more, but exciting.

"Then what?" I wanted him to kiss me again, but I wanted to know more about our future as well.

"We can find somewhere to live nearby. I'd have to stay over at Marstone House some nights, but I'd be at home several nights in the week, at least."

That would have to do—it was no worse than marrying a coachman or the like.

"Moll—I think his lordship has something in mind for the future. Although you're to train with Mrs Wardle as housekeeper…"

I'd likely be with child before I'd learned enough to take over from her.

"…I don't think he wants you to *be* a housekeeper."

"What, then?" His hand was rubbing my arm, and I was having difficulty concentrating.

"I don't know yet. Something a bit out of the ordinary, I should think. But not dangerous, I made sure of that. I told him—"

"You *told* his lordship…?" I was surprised he still had a position.

He smiled down at me, and we forgot about the future for a while. Then a little sense returned, and I straightened my clothing and tucked my hair back under its cap.

"He's an unusual man to work for, Moll. He won't put up with insolence, but he listens to anyone who has something to say. He doesn't want people working for him who are unwilling, and he looks after them. I had a long talk with Archer. Whatever he wants, he won't make you—us—do anything we're not happy with."

"That's all right then." Jem knew his lordship better than I was ever likely to, and I trusted Jem's judgement on that.

"So will you marry me, Molly?"

"After all that kissing, I think I'd better."

He grinned at me "Shall we walk for a bit longer?"

We did, and of course walking wasn't the only thing he had in mind.

I told my lady that evening when I was undressing her, but I think she already knew.

"I'll miss you, Molly. I wouldn't have ended up here, and happy, without your help."

"I think you'd have managed, my lady." I was pleased she'd said that, though.

"You'll give me time to find a new maid, I hope?"

"Of course I will." As long as she didn't take too long about it. A month or so, perhaps—there were the banns to be read, and arrangements to make with the vicar at Over Minster. I wanted to be married where my family would be able to come to the wedding.

My lady said Jem could go back to London with me and the valet in the luggage coach. It was a fine day when we set out, and the two of us decided to sit outside—as we'd done when we tried to get to Devonshire. It was lovely being able to sit close, with his arm around me, while we talked about what his lordship might want us to do.

At the moment I didn't care about that part of the future—it was enough to be sitting with Jem in the sunshine, with the prospect of being with him every day.

EPILOGUE

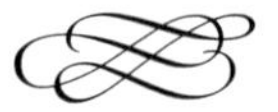

And so here I am, five years later, with two sturdy lads playing in the next room and Jem due to return this evening. He has to stay at Marstone House three nights a week, but that still leaves him plenty of time to spend with his family.

It's a fine lodging house, only a mile from Grosvenor Square, and the training I got from Mrs Wardle has stood me in good stead even though this place is considerably smaller than Marstone House. I've maids to help me run it and look after our boys, as well as a cook and a manservant. They're all very competent, but the main reason his lordship employs them is that they can keep their mouths shut when necessary. Talk about running the house is fine, or their families, or even the price of fish—but not a word to anyone outside the house about our lodgers. Sprout is still running messages, but now he's dressed in rags as a disguise, not out of necessity, and his mother takes in mending, not men.

We have a very exclusive set of lodgers—all sent by Lord Marstone. Some never set foot outside their room, a few are in need of a doctor when they arrive, and his lordship sends someone to care for them when necessary. Some come and go like normal folk. I never know if the names they give me are their real names—it's not my business to know, and that's fine with me.

What is even finer is the way I'm feeling sick again—I hope it's a little girl this time.

THE END

HISTORICAL NOTES

The daily life of servants

I had a bit of difficulty finding out about the details of servants' daily lives in 1782. Two of the most helpful books were *The Complete Servant* by Samuel & Sarah Adams, published in 1825, and *The Duties of a Lady's Maid,* also from 1825 (both these are available as free pdfs from Google Books, if you are interested).

I have some other books about life below stairs in the Victorian and Edwardian eras, and not much appears to have changed over the century. So I thought it was reasonable to assume that not all that much had changed in the forty years or so between Molly's story and 1825.

The main difference, I suspect, would have been in meal times, as the fashionable hour for dinner for the gentry and aristocracy moved from around 3 pm in 1730 to some time between 5 and 7 pm by 1800. I think these times are what are often referred to as 'country hours', and during the season in London, dinners would have been much later.

As the lives of servants revolved around the lives of their employers, the changing fashion for meal times would have affected their own timetables. Molly refers to her dinner a few times in the story—

the servants' dinner was their main meal of the day, and was eaten in the middle of the day, in contrast to their employers' main meal in the evening.

Literacy amongst servants

A couple of early readers were surprised that both Molly and Jem could read and write (although Jem's skills are considerably better than Molly's). Statistics about literacy in the past have to be treated with caution, as at one point merely being able to sign one's name instead of putting an X counted as being literate. Also, being able to read didn't necessarily mean that the person could also write.

Reading was becoming increasingly common amongst the lower classes, particularly those involved in trade (Jem's background). However, rather than take my guidance from academic texts, I have again used *The Duties of a Lady's Maid,* and a similar book, *The Footman's Directory and Butler's Remembrancer,* published in 1823. Although later than my story, I think they are a reasonable guide.

There must have been an expectation that lady's maids and footmen could read, otherwise why publish a book of advice for them? In the lady's maid book, there is a section on amusements in which the author cautions the reader against reading novels 'which have led many a girl to ruin', and recommends improving works and books of practical advice. Indeed, there are so many receipts (the old term for recipes) for skin lotions, mixtures for removing stains from fabrics, and so on, that a maid would have difficulty remembering them all and must have relied on some form of notes or reference book.

Similarly the book for footmen advises them to keep a small notebook to write down who they call on with their employers and where they live, and the names and addresses on cards left at the house—all this to enable them to deliver notes efficiently or lead ladies they are accompanying to the correct places.

Silver paper

In Chapter 5, Molly refers to purchases being wrapped in silver paper. This isn't metal foil, which is what we might be referring to today if we said 'silver paper', but it was a precursor to today's tissue paper—the thin, translucent kind, not the type you blow your nose on.

The paper was a brighter white than most white paper at the time, and thin. It may have got its name because it was also used to wrap jewellery and gold and silver items.

Westminster Abbey

The skeleton in a robe that Molly refers to is part of the tomb of Lady Elizabeth Nightingale. It was such an odd thing to see when I was researching what Molly and Bella might see there, that I couldn't resist mentioning it in the story.

Fashion dolls and fashion plates

The fashion dolls referred to in the story were also known as Pandora dolls. This story takes place just before the first fashion magazines became popular, so dolls were still used to give customers an indication of both styles and fabrics. Once fashion magazines were in wider circulation, the fashion plates more commonly referred to in stories of the period took the place of dolls.

AFTERWORD

Thank you for reading *Molly's Tale*; I hope you enjoyed it. If you can spare a few minutes, I'd be very grateful if you could review this book on Amazon or Goodreads.

Find out more about the Marstone Series, as well as my other books, on the following pages or on my website.

www.jaynedavisromance.co.uk

If you want news of special offers or new releases, join my mailing list via the contact page on my website. I won't bombard you with emails, I promise! Alternatively, follow me on Facebook - links are on my website.

ABOUT THE AUTHOR

I wanted to be a writer when I was in my teens, hooked on Jane Austen and Georgette Heyer (and lots of other authors). Real life intervened, and I had several careers, including as a non-fiction author under another name. That wasn't *quite* the writing career I had in mind!

Now I am lucky enough to be able to spend most of my time writing, when I'm not out walking, cycling, or enjoying my garden.

THE MARSTONE SERIES

A duelling viscount, a courageous poor relation and an overbearing lord–just a few of the memorable cast of characters you will meet in *The Marstone Series*. From windswept Devonshire, to Georgian London and revolutionary France, true love is always on the horizon and shady dealings often afoot.

Each book can be read as a standalone story, but readers of the series will enjoy meeting characters from previous books. They are available as individual novels in ebook and paperback. The full-length novels are also available as a box set in ebook only.

A Question of Duty - Book 0 (Prequel Novella)

Sauce for the Gander - Book 1

A Winning Trick - Book 1.5 (Extended epilogue to Book 1)

A Suitable Match - Book 2

Molly's Tale - Book 2.5 (Companion novel to Book 2)

Playing with Fire - Book 3

The Fourth Marchioness - Book 4

ALSO BY JAYNE DAVIS

THE MRS MACKINNONS

England, 1799

Major Matthew Southam returns from India, hoping to put the trauma of war behind him and forget his past. Instead, he finds a derelict estate and a family who wish he'd died abroad.

Charlotte MacKinnon married without love to avoid her father's unpleasant choice of husband. Now a widow with a young son, she lives in a small Cotswold village with only the money she earns by her writing.

Matthew is haunted by his past, and Charlotte is fearful of her father's renewed meddling in her future. After a disastrous first meeting, can they help each other find happiness?

Available on Kindle and in paperback. Read free in Kindle Unlimited. Listen via Audible or AudioBooks.com.

AN EMBROIDERED SPOON

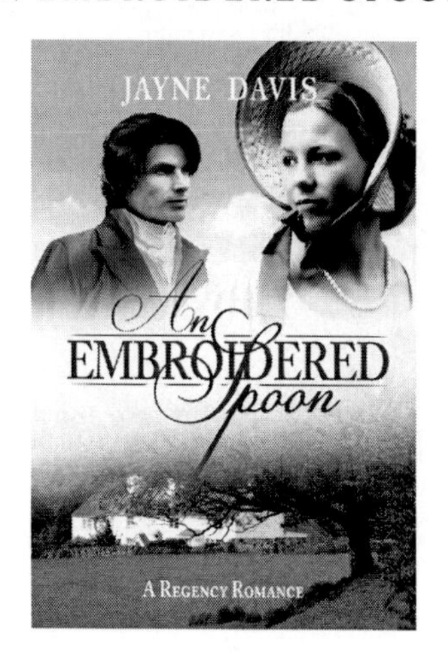

Can love bridge a class divide?

Wales 1817

After refusing every offer of marriage that comes her way, Isolde Farrington is packed off to a spinster aunt in Wales until she comes to her senses.

Rhys Williams, there on business, is turning over his uncle's choice of bride for him, and the last thing he needs is to fall for an impertinent miss like Izzy – who takes Rhys for a yokel. But while a man may choose his wife, he cannot choose who he falls in love with.

Izzy's new surroundings make her look at life, and Rhys, afresh. As she realises her early impressions were mistaken, her feelings about him begin to change. But when her father, Lord Bedley, discovers the situation in Wales is not what he thought, and that Rhys is in trade, Izzy is hurriedly returned to London. Will a difference in class keep them apart?

Available on Kindle and in paperback. Read free in Kindle Unlimited. Listen via most retailers of audio books.

CAPTAIN KEMPTON'S CHRISTMAS

A sweet, second-chance novella.

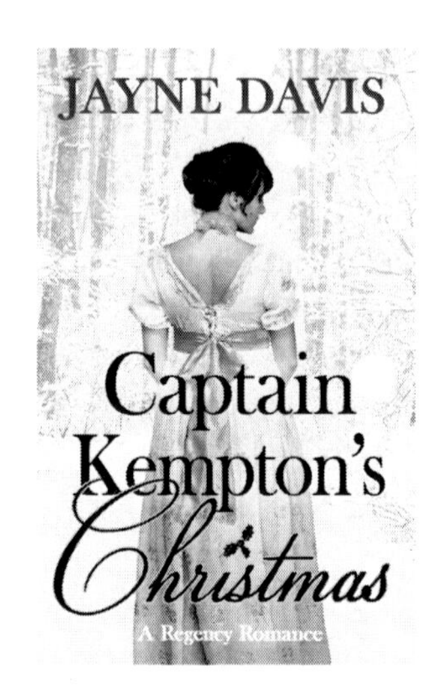

Can broken promises ever be forgiven?

England 1814

Lieutenant Philip Kempton and Anna Tremayne fall in love during one idyllic summer fortnight.

When he's summoned to rejoin his ship, Anna promises to wait for him. While he's at sea, she marries someone else.

Four years later, he is a captain and she is a widow. When the two are forced together at a Christmas party, they have a chance to reconcile.

Can they forgive each other the past and rekindle their love?

Available on Kindle and in paperback. Read free in Kindle Unlimited.

SAVING MEG

A soldier returns to keep a promise—but it will prove more difficult than he imagined.

When Lieutenant Jonathan Lewis' best friend, Fred, is fatally injured on the battlefield. He promises to take care of Fred's sister and mother—after all, he has been quietly in love with Fred's sister, Meg, for years.

Jon finally returns to find England in the grip of a snowy winter. Thoughts of Meg have kept him going, but when he reaches her home, it is not Meg who meets him at the door but her cousin Rupert. Jon is devastated to learn that Rupert and Meg are to be wed in two days' time.

Despite Rupert's efforts to keep them apart, Jon manages to talk to Meg, who does *not* want to marry her cousin. Jon sets off through the icy conditions and deep snow to get a marriage licence before Rupert can force Meg to marry him. But does Meg only want him for her safety, or could she love him, too? And can he make it back in time?

Available on Kindle and in paperback. Read free in Kindle Unlimited.

Made in United States
North Haven, CT
24 July 2023